FEBRUARY DRAGON

Also by Colin Thiele

BLUE FIN
FIRE IN THE STONE
FIGHT AGAINST ALBATROSS TWO

FEBRUARY DRAGON

by Colin Thiele

Harper & Row, Publishers

New York, Hagerstown, San Francisco, London

Library of Congress Cataloging in Publication Data
Thiele, Colin.
    February Dragon.

    SUMMARY: The lives of three Australian children are cruelly affected when a bushfire known as the February Dragon sweeps across the countryside.
    [1. Forest fires—Fiction. 2. Australia—Fiction]
I. Title.
PZ7.T354Fe8   [Fic]   76-7879
ISBN 0-06-026092-0
ISBN 0-06-026093-9 lib. bdg.

CONTENTS

Old Barnacle's store

Resin, Turps, and Columbine—who despite his nickname was a boy—stood on tiptoe at the shop counter, waiting eagerly.

"Aniseed balls," Resin said. "Sixpence worth of aniseed balls, please."

Old Barnacle looked down at the three children suspiciously.

"So, it's aniseed balls this time, is it?"

He carried the stepladder across from the other side of the shop and stood it against the steep wooden shelves.

"Last time it was chewing gum, and the time before that it was jelly beans, and the time before that licorice allsorts." He started climbing slowly up the ladder. "By rights I shouldn't serve you, not with stuff like that. Rots your teeth and sugars up your works."

"Does it?" Resin asked archly.

1

Old Barnacle paused on the third rung and looked back at him severely. "Of course it does. Anybody knows that. Hasn't your teacher told you?"

"No."

All three looked at him innocently, bug-eyed.

"Who's your teacher?" Barnacle asked.

"Miss Strarvy-Lemmen."

"What a name!"

Barnacle started to climb higher up the ladder. Whether he really knew that Resin and Turps had been trying to say "Miss Strarvy" while little Columbine had squeaked "Miss Lemon" they couldn't guess. The old shopkeeper was as sharp as a possum's tooth under his crusty cover, and everyone suspected that he knew much more than he wanted people to think.

"Well, she ought to tell you about your teeth."

Turps leaned forward on the counter and stretched her bare feet far out behind her. "It wouldn't be much fun, though, if you couldn't eat sugar at all, Mr. Billings."

"Do you the world of good."

But the old man's tone softened as it always did when someone called him "Mr. Billings." Turps was shrewd enough to know this, so she avoided his nickname. Yet to everyone else in the district Mr. Barney Billings, merchant and storekeeper, didn't exist. He had become "Old Barnacle Bill" so many years ago that few people could remember his real name. Turps rubbed one bare leg against the other like a human grasshopper.

"They say it's good for you, gives you energy."

"What does?"

"Sugar."

"Who says?"

"Miss Strarvy."

"Huh." It was a kind of airy snort in his throat. The old man climbed the ladder until he could reach up and grab one of the glass jars on the sweets shelf. Then, very deliberately, he descended, put the jar on the counter, and took off the lid.

"Sixpence worth?"

"Yes. . . . Please."

Resin waited expectantly, while Turps rubbed the shin of her left leg high across the back of her right thigh, like a violinist playing behind his back. There was silence for a while, except for the clicking of the aniseed balls as they were counted out and dropped into the little white paper bag. "Twenty-one . . . twenty-two . . . twenty-three . . . twenty-four. . . ." A rustling of paper as the top was folded in. "There you are, Resin."

"Thanks."

"Sixpence." The hot, grubby sixpence changed hands and dropped into the till.

"How did you earn it this time? Cleaning out the fowl shed?"

"No, helping Miss Lemon."

"Oh."

"And Miss Strarvy."

"Sounds as though those two get on very well."

Resin grinned. "They do. Very."

Old Barnacle put the lid back and laboriously replaced the jar on the high shelf, where it stood stiff and still, like a glass barrel of toy cannonballs side by side, with a dozen similar jars standing to attention over piles of licorice allsorts, almond rock, boiled mints, faded green jubes, sharp white peppermints stamped with

3

crowns, caramels, minties, fruit pastilles, and lollipops with interesting messages on them: "I love you"; "U.R. mine"; "Blast off"; and "You're my planet, Janet."

"Now, Turps," Barnacle said, when he came down to the counter again, dusting his hands and flicking his old apron. "What do you want?"

"Threepence worth of aniseed balls, please."

Old Barnacle stiffened angrily. "Well, why the blazes didn't you say so when I had the jar down the first time?" He stamped up the ladder, rumbling to himself. "Silly little flitter-bats, they never think further than their noses." He seized the jar, climbed down, thumped it in front of them, and counted out the right number, throwing them into the bag sharply so that they clicked and cracked together like glass beads. "Ten, eleven, twelve." He handed Turps the bag, took her money, and turned to Columbine sternly. "And now *you*, do *you* want three-pence worth of aniseed balls too?"

"No, thanks," little Columbine said, staring up at him blandly. "I want . . ."

"Good," Barnacle said roughly.

"I want . . ."

"Then at least we know where we stand." He took the jar and climbed up to replace it on the shelf. "Not like your silly sister.

"Yes, but I . . ."

"Why she couldn't speak up in the first place I don't know." He came down panting and puffing from exertion, put his huge hands on the counter in front of Columbine, and looked at him sharply. "Well now, what do *you* want?"

"I . . . I . . ." Columbine started uncertainly in a dormouse's voice. "I've only got a . . . a . . ."

4

He choked, looked up at the Fee-fi-fo-fum giant towering over him, and then said it all in a tumbling rush. "I want-a-pennyworth-of-aniseed-balls."

Old Barnacle's face blackened like a thundercloud. "Out!" he roared, pointing to the door and bringing his six-pound boot down on the wooden floor with such a crash that the shelves shook and three loose onions bounced off the counter. "Out of the shop!"

"But . . . but . . . " Poor Columbine was close to tears. "I-I want my aniseed b- . . . "

"Cheeky pests! Think you can give me the tuppenny climb! Pennyworth, tuppenceworth, threepenceworth. Get out!"

"But I want my ani- . . . "

"Here," Resin consoled him, as he led him hastily to the door. "Take eight of mine; that's twice as many as you would have got for your own penny anyway." Then, thinking to save something out of the transaction, he added, "You can give *me* your penny."

"And don't come back!" roared Barnacle. "My legs are worn short with climbing, all for the sake of sugar lickers like *you*." He thumped the counter. "Pines! Pines—with your silly nicknames. Turps and Resin and Columbine—just because your name is Pine. Get out and never come back."

They knew he really didn't mean it, though they had often wondered why he didn't keep his jars on the counter with the eggs and the onions, instead of standing them so high up out of reach. But no doubt he had a reason.

Old Barnacle's store stood at the side of the dusty road that ran from Summertown to Upper Gumbowie. A sprawling, ramshackle, delicious old store it was, dim and untidy inside, and crowded with everything that was ever made. The children loved it. As soon as they pushed open the warped screen door and pressed their bare feet on the worn grain and knotty little knolls of the wooden floorboards, they were walking in a different world. It was a world that smelled of onions and harness leather; camphor balls, pepper, and sour cucumbers. A world littered and cluttered with magic: rabbit traps and jams, axes, saws, sprockets, and eggs; slabs of bacon, cans of molasses and paint, pens, marshmallows, and rope; long straight sausages and heavy-heeled working boots; open bags of sugar with half-swallowed scoops in their throats; butter, bolts, mixed biscuits, and salt; cans of herring and tomato sauce; jars of honey and bottles of brightly colored cordials and essences; sweets, saucepans, vinegar, currants, clocks, shirts, fleecy-lined pajamas, carbolic acid, cod-liver oil; and all the wonderful tastes, smells, surprises, and dreams that lay unknown in hidden cupboards and on dark mysterious shelves.

In the two little dim display windows, the blowflies buzzed monotonously up and down against the glass, or lay silently on their backs with their legs in the air. At one end of the counter stood a row of pigeonholes, a pair of scales, an inkstand, and a mess of papers—blotters, booklets, stamp pads, and old envelopes. This was the Post Office, and somewhere in the midst of all this, at the counter, behind the groceries, among the hardware, out through the back door, on the veranda, or halfway up the shelves, you would always find Old Barnacle. He never seemed to leave the place. He was as permanent as the daddy-long-legs spiders, and the strange, sweet-sour smells that lived in the store forever. He was gruff and grumpy, crusty and cranky, shrewd and kind, all at once, and he

6

knew every boy and girl in the district better than their own fathers did.

That was why Turps just laughed when they were ordered out of the shop. "Never mind, Columbine," she said. "He'll be all right again tomorrow."

"But I tried to tell him I only had a penny. He wou- . . . he wouldn't listen to me."

"Poor old Barnacle, he must have a bone in his leg today." Turps took an aniseed ball out of her mouth to examine the way it was changing color, and sucked it back in again like a vacuum cleaner. "Come on! Mum'll be waiting." Holding Columbine's hand, she led the way across the road and up the slope toward their house.

Pets

Not far from Old Barnacle's store Resin, Turps, and
Columbine lived in a wide, shady house at the end of the
scrub. The gum trees and wattles, blackbutts, she-oaks,
and native pines came jostling down the slope almost to
the back door. Then, just as it looked as though they were
going to trample over the farmyard and the sheds and
Mrs. Pine's vegetable garden, they sidestepped, and
veered off along the edges of the cleared land, sweeping
and tossing their leaves and branches in the spring wind.
People called the uncleared land "The Big Scrub." It
stretched far off toward the South Australian border, except where it was broken up by farms or roads or telephone lines. Everyone called the house "Bottlebrush
Barn," which was the name Dad gave to the shack he had
built there after the war, when he first started clearing
the land.

A little later, when he married, he had built the shady house, with the great vines climbing up the verandas, but it was still called Bottlebrush Barn. Sometimes their mother scolded about the name. "Harry Pine," she'd say, "I wish you would stop calling the place a barn. What must people think?" But Dad laughed. "It's a good name," he'd say, "and everybody knows it, so let it stay." And it stayed.

The nearest school was fifteen miles away in Upper Gumbowie, and the narrow road from the Barn twisted and ducked among the trees, swept down into creek beds, panted over ridges, shot along straight fences past farms and clearings, and finally looped happily into the town. In the mornings the school bus rattled and darted, and stopped and started, for fifteen miles, on its way southward along the road, and in the afternoons it rattled and darted, and stopped and started, fifteen miles back again.

It always spent the night at George Dobson's farmhouse, about a mile up the road from Bottlebrush Barn, because that was where Miss Strarvy lived. He was the teacher who drove the bus. His real name was Mr. Harvey, but people never seemed to have time to pause between the "Mr." and the "Harvey" when they were speaking, so they made "Miss Strarvy" out of it.

At twenty to eight every morning the bus started with a terrifying snort, and wobbled off slowly out of a cloud of smoke, rinsed with blue in the early sunlight. Mr. and Mrs. Dobson's two children, Don and Debby, sat with their knees up on the backseat. Miss Strarvy pumped the accelerator and the choke, grazed the big strainer post by the farmyard gate, and careered down the road, straightening his coat collar with his left hand as he drove along, and whistling "Waltzing Matilda" so loudly that his lips looked like the underside of a mushroom. At Bottlebrush Barn he stopped with a lurch, calling out "Good morning, everyone" in a cheerful voice, long before Resin, Turps, and Columbine could get on the bus. "Morning, sir," they'd say in a chorus, and walk with big strides down the center of the bus to join the other two at the back.

Resin, whose real name was Melton, was nearly twelve —big and tawny-haired, he liked wearing long pants and an old Army slouch hat that Dad had brought back from the war. Dad was proud of Resin. "Be running the farm in a year or two," he'd say. "Reckon I can retire then." Turps, who had been christened Crystal, was ten—bright-eyed and spindle-shanked. And little Colin, whom everyone called Columbine instead of Colin Pine, was only six. Resin had started junior-high work; Turps, Don, and Debby were all in the same elementary grade; and little Columbine was still in kindergarten.

And so Miss Strarvy's bus whooped happily through the trees or ground the teeth of its gears up the ridges, collecting more and more children from the gates and corners and tracks and milk shelters until the seats were crowded. Brenda Wilson was there, and Bridget and Bill O'Brien, and the Hammond children, and Burp Heaslip, and a dozen more. Burp's name was really "Bert," but once when Columbine was just a toddler and couldn't talk properly, he'd called him "Burp" and everyone had laughed so much that the name had stuck. Luckily Burp didn't mind at all. He had a freckled face as round as a tin plate with rust spots all over it, and he always laughed or grinned about nothing at all.

"Here we are," Miss Strarvy would say as the bus rollicked up the road to the Upper Gumbowie School. "Five minutes before bell time." And everyone would shoot out onto the footpath like gravel from a dump truck.

All through the day they worked side by side with the children from Upper Gumbowie, just as if they all lived together in the town. But at four o'clock the bus travelers split up again and rushed outside to wait for Miss Strarvy, and by five o'clock they were being unloaded at the end of the run, dropped off onto the dusty road like sacks with legs. Soon only the Pines and the Dobsons were left. Then Resin, Turps, and Columbine clattered off, and Don and Debby were alone for the last mile to their home, where the bus and Miss Strarvy rested again until the next morning.

Bottlebrush Barn was a wonderful place for pets. To begin with, there was a huge black mountain of a mongrel tomcat, two feet long and one foot high, called "Puss'll-do." He had somehow been left with this queer name years before, when no one could suggest what the new black kitten should be called. Eventually they had turned to Mr. Pine.

"Dad, you give him a name. No matter what you call him, we'll agree with you."

"Oh, Puss'll do," Dad had said casually, and so Puss'll-do it was, and Puss'll-do it had remained.

As well as the big black tomcat there were three dogs on the farm, five calves, two pet lambs, thirteen piglets, half a dozen goats, a pair of black rabbits, four other cats, two ferrets, and a cockatoo. Admittedly the calves were not really house pets, but Resin and Turps had to help feed them, and so they christened each one and spoke of it as part of the farmyard.

In addition to the dozens of usual pets—the ones Resin

11

called "regulars"—there were two outsiders. One was Jacky, the kookaburra, who turned up once or twice a week at daybreak and flew straight at Mrs. Pine's bedroom window. It was a signal to let everyone in the house know that he was hungry and that it was time to get up. He struck the glass with such a crash, it made the frame creak and brought Mr. Pine leaping out of bed like a thunderclap.

"All right, all right," he'd yell. "Blast it all, there's no need to smash the window!" And he'd quickly get some juicy lumps of meat from the refrigerator and throw them out by the kitchen door. For a while nothing would happen. The trees would sigh, and the wind nudge lightly about the house. Then there would be a shadowy rush of brown wings in the dim light as Jacky came swooping in to snatch up the morsels. A moment later he would be gone again in a blur, and there would suddenly be a new stump of wood, sitting quite motionless, high up on the branch of a nearby tree. As the daylight grew, Jacky would think things over for a while until the idea of Mr. Pine leaping out of bed in his pajamas tickled his fancy so much that he would fling back his head and laugh till the hillside rang, and the feathers under his open beak shook as if he were gargling his throat with the light from the rising sun. At last, when he had finished his joke, he flew away silently, and nobody saw him again for three or four days.

The other outsider was Gus. He came and went even more secretly than Jacky. But five or six times a year somebody was sure to stumble on him with a start and a thrill of surprise, and race up to the house, yelling, "Hey, Gus is back, I just saw him—he's as big as a croc!" Mrs. Pine wasn't quite so keen about Gus as the others were. For Gus was a goanna, a big bull bush goanna, five feet long. He had a body like an alligator's, a long tapering tail, a slim neck with a shovel head, and four strong legs. In the summer they would sometimes see him drinking at the cattle trough, or lying in the damp shade of a cucumber patch by the dam, and now and again someone would get a surprise to find him basking in the spring sunshine behind the haystack.

When this happened to the children, they would always jump. "Ooh, gosh!" Then, a second later, "Ah-h, it's only Gus. Hullo Gus." Gus would raise himself slowly on all four feet until he seemed to be balancing on his claws like a dancer, his head darting gently and his eyes flashing. "It's all right, Gus. No need to be frightened." That was a joke really, because Resin and Turps, and especially young Columbine, were just as uncertain and suspicious about Gus, with his strong teeth and claws, as Gus seemed to be about them.

Then a dog would bark, or a horse stamp nearby, and Gus would be off like a rocket in a flurry of straw and whirling sticks, sweeping up toward The Big Scrub as swiftly as a long thick shadow.

"Sneaky reptile," their mother said. "I wouldn't trust that fellow any more than a fox or a ferret."

"Oh, Mum! Gus wouldn't do a thing. Honest."

Their mother mimicked them nastily.

"Oh, no, Gus wouldn't do a thing, except snoop around the fowl shed, sniffing out the eggs and little chickens with that great long tongue of his."

"But, Mum, he's a pet."

"Well, then let's bring him in by the fire like a cat and stroke his ugly scaly back every night."

"He is a pet. He knows we wouldn't hurt him."

13

"I'll hurt him all right if I catch him stealing my eggs. I'll take the broomstick to him." Mr. Pine laughed at that. "Leave him alone, Mum," he said; "as long as he's about, we won't be bothered with snakes."

That was how Gus got the run of Bottlebrush Barn. All except for the house and the verandas. He seemed to know that if he ventured out of the vegetable garden up to the back door, Mrs. Pine would take to him with the broomstick.

The Dragon

Sometimes tourists traveling between Adelaide and Melbourne used the road past Bottlebrush Barn for their cars and trailers. It was good, they said, to get off the main highways for a change and to see Australia by the back roads and bush tracks. But most of them didn't really see Australia at all. They swept past with engines roaring, tires whirring, and radios blaring, so that they never had a chance to see the sun shining through the green fern in the creek, or to feel the soft tickle of moss on a log with the tips of their fingers, or to smell the faint scent of a wild flower as small as a spider's eye, or to hear the talk of crickets under the bark, or the itching and clicking of insects like beetles' castanets at the end of a still summer day.

And if a cat, or possum, or rabbit didn't get out of the way, cars rushed down on them, crushing them or tossing them aside in the grass, maimed and bleeding. It was worse at night than by day. The headlights came boring through the darkness, dazzling and terrifying the animals, freezing them into statues until destruction thundered down on them.

Sometimes on a fine Sunday night Resin, Turps, and Columbine would sit with their parents on the veranda. Now and again a car would sweep past the front gate and disappear, with its taillights glaring angrily, down the road past old Barnacle's store.

One night as they watched, a strange thing happened. A red bullet seemed to shoot out from a passing car and whizz through the air, scattering sparks like fireworks. It hit the road and leaped off in a lovely shower of red streamers into the bush, where it stopped spinning at last and lay quite still like a tiny firefly, winking and glowing for a long time until it faded and disappeared.

"Ooh, whatever was that?" Turps yelled. "Wasn't it beautiful!"

Her father looked serious.

"It may have been beautiful," he said, "but it was the most dangerous thing in Australia."

Turps looked puzzled. "Why, Dad?"

"Because of what it was."

"What was it?"

"Fire."

"Fire?"

"A cigarette butt."

Turps was astonished. "It couldn't have been. It looked like fireworks."

"It could have given us fireworks all right," her father said ominously. "Enough to supply South Australia and Victoria too. It could have set the whole countryside alight, turned the gum trees into torches, the pines into giant sparklers, and the hillsides into rivers of fire."

"Bushfires?"

"Bushfires."

"How horrible."

Mrs. Pine straightened her knitting. Then she looked up.

"People shouldn't be allowed to throw their cigarettes and matches out of passing cars. Don't they know there's a law against it?"

Mr. Pine swatted at a mosquito.

"People are careless, Muriel. They forget they're in the bush, and they just toss out their butts as though they're driving down St. Kilda Road or over Sydney Harbor Bridge." He sighed. "Ah well, I suppose it keeps all of us on our toes, especially the E.F.S."

Resin knew well enough what that meant. He had seen the men of the Emergency Fire Service training at Upper Gumbowie. The members were ordinary men: shearers and wheat growers, truck drivers, clerks, and shopkeepers from the farms and little towns, who dropped everything and rushed off in the fire trucks whenever an alarm sounded. They spread the news by telephone, wireless, and sirens, until men came pouring toward the fire from every farm and township for miles around.

"Fires start in hundreds of ways," Mr. Pine said, "but almost always from human beings, and almost always from carelessness. Campfires, broken exhaust pipes, bad spark plugs on tractors and railway trains, magnifying glasses and empty bottles, hot ashes, incinerators, welding gear, lamps, electrical faults. But most of all from silly people with cigarettes and matches." He sat silently again for a minute.

17

"They don't realize that a match is nothing but a chained-up dragon. If once they let him loose, he is likely to wipe out everything for a hundred miles around."

Turps put her arms high up around her knees and shuddered. She had never thought of a match as a chained-up dragon before.

Woppit

In spite of the surprises and excitement that Gus and Jacky sometimes caused, it was one of the dogs that accidentally provided the most hair-raising incident of all. He was Woppit, an inoffensive old fellow, half kangaroo dog, half kelpie, who had been working on the farm for ten or twelve years. According to Mr. Pine he should have been pensioned off long ago, but he was still much too energetic for that. Because of his kangaroo-dog blood he could still run faster over a short distance than either of the other two dogs, Snap and Blue, and he seemed to have eyes like telescopes because, once they had seen a rabbit or a hare, they locked onto it and never lost sight of it again. As he grew older, Woppit's coat got thinner and more moth-eaten every day.

"Losing his fur, that dog of yours, ain't he, Harry?" George Dobson said to Mr. Pine one day. "Looks as if the mice have been at it."

"Yes, it's getting kind of scurfy," Mr. Pine admitted. "Must be old age."

"By yiminy, 'Arry," old Emil Eckert, their German neighbor, crowed a couple of days later, "dat dog don't grow much of a crop of hair. Never have I seen anudder dog mit a worse crop dan dat."

"It's not very thick," Mr. Pine agreed.

"Tick? Is not tick at all. Is tin, very tin."

"It is thin, I guess."

"Never haff I a tinner crop in my life seen. I t'ink d' drought he is having on his back. Notting vill grow dere no more."

"Well, there's nothing I can do about it," Mr. Pine said. "I'm not going to put hair restorer on his back."

Old Emil pushed back his felt hat and laughed. "I t'ink you better put super on it, or blood-and-bone manure perhaps."

But Mr. Pine wasn't inclined to treat it as such a joke. "A watering with the garden hose is all he's likely to get," he said, "or maybe a good wash with soap and warm water."

"Dat vill not do much good," Emil insisted. "Look at you. You is all d' time voshing your head mit soapy water, but you is getting balder every day."

Although some of the neighbors kept on laughing at poor Woppit's coat, the Pine children were worried about it. Turps, especially, began to get angry when their friends on the school-bus run joined in and started asking whether Woppit had red rust or dandruff in his hair. A week or two later a small sore appeared on Woppit's back and Turps was really alarmed.

"There's something wrong with him," she said emphatically. "He's got a disease."

20

Resin agreed with her. "A skin disease. Dermatitis or something."

But their father wasn't very sympathetic. "Don't be so silly. It's not a skin disease."

"Why isn't it?"

"Because he's quite happy and comfortable. You don't see him scratching himself or rubbing his back against a post, do you?"

"No."

"Well, then, it can't be hurting or itching."

"He might be very strong-willed."

"So might my aunty."

"I still think we ought to take him to a vet."

But their father reacted very strongly to that idea. "A vet? Where do you think the nearest vet is?"

"In Summertown?"

"Yes. And I'm certainly not going to drive sixty miles in the middle of the plowing just because an old crock of a dog gets a scratch on his back."

"He's not an old crock! He's Woppit!"

"He'll be better in a week or two. Probably got a nip in a fight."

The children gave up the argument then, but they were not convinced. They decided to keep a close watch on old Woppit and to act quickly if he grew worse.

The following Saturday Mrs. Pine was seized with one of her periodic fits of spring-cleaning. It was a beautiful morning, calm and sunny. Mrs. Pine threw open both the front and back doors so that the clean air could march through the house down the main corridor, and frolic in and out through the windows, chimneys, and ventilators.

"Nothing like a good spring-cleaning to blow the cob-

21

webs away and freshen things up a bit," she said.

Resin had escaped into The Big Scrub with his father to look for likely fence-post timber, but Turps and Columbine were in the thick of it. They brushed, scrubbed, swept, and beat until their arms ached, but their mother never paused. Five or six times they staggered out to the rubbish heap with loads of unwanted junk. Packing cases, old boots and shoes, pictures and calendars, cracked dishes, almanacs, empty flagons and bottles, cans of all shapes and sizes, piles of newspapers and magazines, an old meat cooler, cardboard boxes, wrapping paper, broken knife blades, useless toys, the confusion of bric-a-brac hoarded by everyone for years—all went out onto the dump.

"Anyone would think it was a nest for lyrebirds," their mother said a little breathlessly. "It's high time we had a good clean-out." She wielded the mop and buzzed the vacuum cleaner until the carpets were as clean and soft to the touch as a cat's fur, and the linoleum was a patterned mirror. From time to time Mrs. Pine stood back to admire everything. It was clear that she was proud of the result of her work.

Twice Turps and Columbine had to go down to Old Barnacle's store for new supplies of floor wax and brass polish. And it was on the second of these trips that the great Woppit Incident took place. Old Barnacle started it.

"Nice dog you've got there," he said, leaning over the counter and almost smiling. Turps was so surprised at this sudden and unexpected show of friendliness that she looked up quickly, suspicious that the old man had joined all the other people of the district and was really ridiculing Woppit. But Barnacle was quite serious. Turps warmed to him.

22

"Do you think so?" she asked, smiling.

"Of course. Seen him with your father; always liked him."

"Have you?"

"Good cut of a dog. Fast. Got a bit of kangaroo dog in him."

Turps beamed. It was one of Barnacle's rare happy days. And, although he would never admit it, he secretly liked Turps.

"Must've been a great farm dog in his time, eh?"

"Oh, yes. Wonderful."

"Clever, eh?"

"Oh, very clever. Still is."

Columbine hastened to support his sister. "He's cleverer than Snap or Bluey. Dad says he's never had a cleverer dog than Woppit." They all stood in silent admiration for a while. Then Turps' face fell. "But he's getting old. And his coat's awfully . . . well, sort of scruffy-looking."

Barnacle pooh-poohed her concern. "Nothing to worry about."

Columbine looked up at him with big bug eyes. "We think his skin is getting worn out."

Barnacle laughed. "No matter. It's what's inside that counts."

"D'you reckon?"

"Sure of it. Same with people. I don't care whether they're as smooth as babies or as wrinkled as elephants, so long as they're not rotten inside."

Columbine stepped forward earnestly. "Oh, Woppit's not rotten inside!'

"Course he's not. So what are you worrying about?"

Turps patted Woppit's moldy coat. "Well, it's gone quite bald in one patch on his back—see."

Barnacle was concerned. He put on his glasses and came bustling out from behind the counter. "Where? Which patch?"

Turps held Woppit and pointed. "There."

Barnacle bent over, peering at it for a second, and then straightened up, laughing. "Huh!" he said lightly. "A bit of scurf! I can clear it in a minute."

Columbine beamed at him. "How, Mr. Barnacle?"

Barnacle frowned at the nickname, but he let it pass. He was too concerned with remedies for the dog.

"Turps'll fix it," he said.

"How will she?"

"Just a touch on the sore spot ought to do it."

Columbine was mystified and astonished. He turned to his sister, evidently picturing in her a miracle of healing. "Gee, Turps, will it? Really?" He paused, thinking, then turned to Barnacle accusingly. "But she's touched Woppit lots of times, and it hasn't made any difference at all."

Turps suddenly understood and doubled up with laughter. "Not *me*," she shrieked. "Mr. Billings means turpentine—the real stuff, in a bottle."

Barnacle, always pleased at the mention of his real name, joined in the laughter so unexpectedly that Turps and Columbine stopped short and looked at him. Neither of them had ever heard him laugh before.

"I'll get some," he chuckled. "Only take a minute."

Woppit sniffed about the shop while the old storekeeper was outside, as if he sensed that all the enjoyment and activity had something to do with him.

"Now it won't be long, Woppit old doggie," Barnacle said, shuffling back urgently with a bottle of turpentine in his hand. "This is the best cure in the world for scurfy

24

backsides." He shook the bottle as though it was cough mixture. "Better come out onto the veranda; we can see better there.'

They lined up outside, Turps holding Woppit by the collar while Barnacle examined him. The worst spot was a bald patch on the slope of his rump above the tail.

"Now," said Barnacle, "just hold him still for a second while I dab a bit on his back." He uncorked the bottle and took a piece of rag out of his pocket. "Might give him a bit of jip for a second or two, so you better hold him pretty tight."

"What's jip, Mr. Barnacle?" Columbine asked.

Barnacle didn't answer. Perhaps he was too busy; perhaps he considered that anyone who didn't know what jip was didn't deserve being talked to. "Now," he said, "if there's any of them virus germs on poor old Woppity here, there's nothing like turps to burn 'em out. Gets rid of 'em in no time."

He upended the bottle onto the rag. Rather more turpentine than he intended flooded out, soaking the rag and spilling onto the floor.

"Now, Woppity, there's a good dog," he said encouragingly. "This'll do you a world of good." He pressed the rag onto Woppit's back, squeezing it as he did so. Turpentine from the saturated pad ran out on both sides, trickling down Woppit's rump and tail.

"There, that'll soon fix . . . " But Barnacle didn't get any further. For with a wild yelp Woppit took off, wrenching his collar free from Turps' hand and sending poor Columbine flying head over heels off the veranda.

"Whoops!" Barnacle yelled, as if the wind had been knocked out of him; "it must be giving him a bit of jip."

"Gosh!" Turps said.

"What's the matter with him?" Columbine asked, picking himself up.

They both looked at Barnacle. For the second time that day he was laughing. "Hey! Hey! Look at him go! By golly, that dog is fast."

"Is it hurting him?" Turps asked, dismayed.

"Just a bit of jip. He'll soon calm down!"

But it was quite clear that the turpentine was giving Woppit plenty of jip. After catapulting from the veranda he raced around in a series of swooping curves, leaping high like a vaulter and swerving and twisting about in midair, trying to bite his back.

"Poor Woppit," Turps cried. "It must be stinging terribly."

"Won't be long," Barnacle said reassuringly, "and he'll be quiet as a lamb again."

But Woppit didn't get as quiet as a lamb. After rolling over and over in the dirt for a minute, he suddenly straightened up and shot off toward Heaslips' dam. They ran out and watched him going down the track, ears flattened and body arching to the rhythm of his speed. As he reached the dam, he leaped off the bank, plunging headlong into the water with a huge splash. As far as they could make out, he wriggled about furiously in the dam for a minute or two before he floundered out, rolled about in the mud and dirt again, and came rocketing back toward the main road. Turps and Columbine ran out to try to intercept him.

"Woppit! Woppit! Here, boy!" Turps called. For a second Woppit made as if to come toward them, but then the sore on his back must have burned him violently again, because he veered off, tore down into the creek bed nearby, soused himself wildly in a couple of shallow water holes there, and came bounding up the bank again like a maniac.

"Woppit! Woppit!" Turps called, running across the main road to head him off. "Here, Woppit!"

Barnacle stood on his veranda watching the chase. "Must've been more jip in that stuff than I thought," he murmured to himself.

A trailer party had drawn up for lunch on the side of the road by The Big Scrub. There were two cars and two campers. Seven or eight people were moving about preparing lunch. Because it was such a lovely day, they had set up a folding table in the open air. Camp stools were scattered about, a spirit stove was hissing under a billy of water, and food, bottles of sauce, cups, plates, cutlery, and dozens of odds and ends were ready on the table or on the ground nearby. It was a happy picnic scene.

"Woppit! Come back here!" Turps' cry, half angry, half pitying, came to them clearly on the sunny air. They were about to sit down to their meal; a woman was slicing bread and one of the men was bending over the boiling billy, preparing to lift it off to pour the tea.

But at that moment Woppit descended on their camp like a willy-willy.

"Woppit!" Turps' call came too late. The long dingo-colored form swept past the campers, brushed aside camp stools and cartons, shot beneath the table, and leaped over the man at the tea-billy, rising right over his back in a long curving arc that would have done credit to a greyhound. There were shouts and cries on all sides, the collapsible table collapsed, and a sauce bottle smashed against the wheel cap of a trailer in a red splurge.

"Hey!"

27

"Get out!"

"Blast it!"

"Stop that crazy dog!"

The campers ran out onto the road, but the lean brown arrow of Woppit's body had already shot off through the gates of Bottlebrush Barn and was racing up the track with Turps and Columbine in pursuit.

"What's up with that loony dog? He got rabies or something?" The campers stood muttering angrily. "Better look out. He might come back."

But Woppit wasn't interested in campers, tables, billies, or anything except the burn on his back.

"Woppit! Good dog, Woppit!" Turps' cry went hallooing up the track toward the house, calling and cajoling without effect.

Mrs. Pine was busy staining the front doorstep with blacking. She looked up impatiently as she heard Turps' distant voice.

"What are those two doing now! There isn't time to be playing about with the dogs." She raised her voice. "Crystal! What in the world are you d- . . . *Woppit!*" For Woppit had come plummeting in through the back door and was pounding down the passage toward her. His body was a pudding of mud and dirt, matted lumps of wet fur, bits of grass, bark, and debris, and his paws made long skidding mudprints right down the shining length of the polished linoleum.

Mrs. Pine, kneeling at the front door, saw only a long thundering dog's body, led by a low-hung head, slavering tongue, and staring eyes, hurtling down the passage toward her. "Stop!" she screamed, brandishing the black brush above her head. "Stop!"

Woppit stopped. He dug in his forepaws and skidded down the linoleum, leaving claw marks like furrows and tracing a long muddy wake with the wet mop of his tail. Mrs. Pine saw the ruin of her morning's work behind him.

"Out, you beast!" she shouted. "Out! Out!" And she sprang to her feet and charged at Woppit with the brush. Woppit turned and went to flee down the passage again, but at that moment Turps appeared panting at the back door, calling and yelling his name. Poor Woppit probably thought she wanted to put another dose of fire on his back. He balked and leaped sideways into the living room, normally a holy of holies where dogs were never allowed, and now shining with polished furniture and cozy with freshly brushed rugs. But there the burning itch on his back overcame him again and he rolled furiously on the floor, rubbing his muddy back into the clean pile of the carpet with a kind of desperate relish. Mrs. Pine and Turps discovered him there, lolloping about with his legs in the air and his tongue out.

"Woppit!" They both yelled together, Turps triumphant at having finally cornered him, Mrs. Pine horrified at what was happening to her living room. "Get out!" she screamed. "Get out! Get out! Oh, just look at what he's done to the new white rug!"

Woppit righted himself, shook a shower of mud and water over half the room, and stood at bay, panting like an engine.

"Stand away from the door," Mrs. Pine shouted. "He can't get out!"

Woppit leaped past her, thumping his rump against the door frame as he escaped, and fled for the back door. There he collided with Columbine, almost sending him sprawling for the second time that day, and reached the open air again. There for the next half hour he could be seen rolling about in the yard or rubbing his back against posts and railings. But slowly the burn of the turpentine must have eased and faded, for he behaved less and less spectacularly, and after about an hour he flopped down in a dust hole like a fowl and lay there exhausted.

Mrs. Pine was furious. It took her most of the afternoon to rectify the havoc he'd caused, and even then things were never quite the same again. Turps was both heartbroken and angry—heartbroken at the pain she had accidentally caused Woppit, and angry at Old Barnacle for having suggested such a stupid remedy.

Mr. Pine was inclined to be forgiving when he heard about it. "I don't think it'll do Woppit any harm," he said. "The old farmers often used to put axle grease or liniment on horses and cows when I was a boy."

"Yes, but Barnacle should have known better."

"He meant it for the best. I wish I could have seen him when Woppit took off."

"He laughed. It was disgusting."

"I'll tell you what was more disgusting," Mrs. Pine said tartly; "my living-room floor after that muddy horse had galloped about in it."

"Wouldn't you gallop too," Mr. Pine replied with a twinkle in his eye, "if someone put turpentine on your tail?"

"Harry!" Mrs. Pine looked at him warningly. But her husband laughed. "Wouldn't you?" "That's enough!" "I'll tell you one thing: I'll bet Woppit won't go near Barnacle again in a hurry."

He was right. Although the old dog's back slowly

healed—whether from natural causes or from the turpentine treatment nobody knew—Woppit never again set a paw inside Barnacle's store.

And from that day they always regarded one another from a distance.

Ginger

Turps had always wanted a pony of her own. For three or four years she had been pestering her mother and father, especially at Christmastime, but Mr. Pine wouldn't hear of it.

"You're still too small to be roaming around the back country on a horse," he said. "Wait till you're big enough."

But whenever Turps asked him when she was likely to be big enough, he avoided giving her a direct answer and just kept on saying, "We'll see."

That was why she now lay in bed early on the morning of her eleventh birthday, half sick with excitement and expectation, one minute hoping so hard that little thrills and tremors chased one another in strange tickles around her stomach, and the next feeling so certain of disappointment again that she almost willed herself into being miserable.

There was a rule in the Pine family that you didn't get up on your birthday until everyone else had come in to sing "Happy Birthday" and spread cards and presents all over the bed. But sometimes, like this morning, it was an agony when you woke up earlier than everyone else and had to lie there just waiting and listening—and hoping. And this year there hadn't been any indication of what Turps might get. Columbine certainly didn't know anything, because he was hopeless at keeping secrets and would have blabbed it all out. Resin was the opposite —closemouthed like his father. It was impossible to guess from them whether they would even remember her birthday.

Her mother, on the other hand, seemed to be quite open about it, but the presents she hinted at—sewing baskets, books, and roller skates—weren't really the kind to get terribly excited about. Not that she wouldn't be grateful for presents like that; she would. But compared with a horse, a real live horse that answered to its name and carried you on its back, you had to admit that books and baskets were, well, a bit ordinary.

She lay still, hardly breathing, as she heard the floor creak outside her room. It was her father, going to wake Resin and Columbine; she could hear the pad-padding of his bare feet in the passage and the half-awake murmurs of the boys. More silence, more waiting. Then, quite suddenly, her door was thrown open and the whole family burst in, singing and thrusting parcels all around her pillow. She struggled into a sitting position and began to untie the string and wrapping. A ball-point pen and some stationery from Columbine. She kissed him on the cheek with a "thank you, Col," to cover his embarrassment.

A pin and a book from Resin; she gave him a grateful

33

smile because she knew how hard he must have saved for it. The sewing basket from her mother, as she'd expected, with compartments for different kinds of wool and cotton, and a special revolving needle container. And, lastly, a packet marked "Crystal, from Dad," which seemed to have endless layers of paper around it.

Eventually she unwrapped a small box in the center and opened it expectantly. Her face fell for a second, but then it lit up again with excitement and bewilderment. There was nothing but a message inside the box: *Look near the lantana bush.*

Turps leaped out of bed and raced out through the back door in her pajamas. The others followed in a group. She ran across the garden to the lantana, searching feverishly under the close screen of leaves. She didn't quite know what to expect, but the idea was unusual enough to make her tingle with hope and uncertainty.

"What is it, Dad? What's her present?" Columbine kept on saying, so it was clear enough that this was a special secret which Dad had kept to himself. She wondered if Resin knew what it was.

There was another box under the lantana, with another message: *What about the kitchen dresser, then?* Her spirits sank a little at that; perhaps it was a toy or some school things after all.

"Ah-h, gosh, Dad!" she said. "Is this an early morning scavenger hunt or something?"

She ran back to the kitchen, with the others trooping after her. A third box with a third message. Her heart gave a kick and her whole face beamed uncontrollably. *Well, why not the barn?* She tore across the yard to the hay barn. It could just be a joke, of course, but this time she felt there would be no more jokes or tricks.

She reached the barn, snapped open the latch, slid back the heavy door . . . and stood quite still. The others came up behind her. A pony was standing in the middle of the barn, looking at them with round, questioning eyes.

"O-o-oh! Oh, isn't she *beautiful*!" Turps' voice trembled. She was close to tears—tears of delight, of gratitude, of admiration, and joy.

"What's her name?"

Her father came up by Turps' side. "Ginger."

"Ginger! . . . I like that." She turned to the others with shining eyes. "Yes, I love that." She stepped forward slowly with her hand outstretched. "Hullo, Ginger. It's me. I'm Turps."

The mare tossed her head a little but she didn't move away. Instead, as Turps' hand drew near, she bent down her neck and explored it for a second with her velvet nose. Turps patted the nose gently and then slid her hand up to the warm smooth throat and the strong arch of the pony's neck.

"Hullo, Ginger," she kept saying. "I'm your . . . your new mate." The pony nuzzled her and came forward in friendly exploration of the others. "Oh, you're the loveliest thing," Turps burst out, hanging on to her neck and hugging her. "The loveliest, most beautiful thing in the world."

"She's tame, Dad," Columbine said shrilly; "she's tame, isn't she, Dad?"

They all went forward then, to pat and coddle Ginger, until Mrs. Pine called a halt to it. "Come on, you pajama-wearers, back to the house. It'll be broad daylight soon, and here we are still running about undressed." But it took another ten minutes to drag Turps away, and only

35

then by promising she could go for a ride straight after breakfast.

"Is she easy to ride, do you know, Dad?"

"As good as gold once she's warm," her father said; "rode her over from Eckerts' myself last night. But they say she's a bit flighty first thing in the morning."

"She should lose that when she gets a bit older, shouldn't she?" Mrs. Pine asked.

"I guess. She still shies a bit, too."

Columbine looked up questioningly. "What's *shies*, Dad?"

"Gets frightened and jumpy over strange things— things she doesn't understand. You might be riding along as gently as you like, when suddenly she sees a white cat or a rabbit or a shirt flapping on the line, or an old bag or a log—anything that startles her—and *whoosh*, she's off."

"Where to?"

Mr. Pine roared with laughter. "Anywhere. She might stand straight up on her hind legs or jump sideways or stop short so that you go sailing on over her head."

"Gosh!" Columbine was awestruck.

"You'll frighten Turps in a second," Resin said. "She might want to give Ginger away."

"Never!" Turps declared passionately. "We're friends; we know each other already."

It was true. Within a few weeks Turps and her pony were inseparable. They were known throughout the district. Ginger was a beautiful creature—a four-year-old chestnut mare, golden as honey, quick, bright-eyed, and mischievous. The sun seemed to sleep in her glowing coat; and when she galloped down the slope to her stall, with her mane in the wind and her tail streaming, she looked like a golden Pegasus. And in Turps' eyes that was what she was. To Turps, Ginger was a dream and a miracle; and she was both of these because she was a pony.

Of course, there were incidents which occasionally broke up the smooth flow of farm life, and Ginger was usually in the thick of them. Twice she tumbled Columbine from her back, but luckily each time it was in the middle of a fallow paddock and he wasn't hurt; once she stopped short unexpectedly when Resin was trying to coax her to jump a log, so that he left her behind and made the trip through the air on his own.

And then, one day, she dumped poor Burp Heaslip like a bag of barley near the chicken shed. But the real culprit that time was Gus. It was a Saturday afternoon and the children were taking turns riding Ginger, when suddenly a tremendous commotion broke out in the chicken yard. Everyone raced over to see what was the matter, and Burp, whose turn it happened to be, rode after them on Ginger.

The moment they got around to the front of the sheds, there was pandemonium. "It's Gus!" Columbine yelled. "He's got a chicken."

"Hey, drop that!" Resin rushed forward, blocking the doorway and inadvertently cutting off Gus' line of escape. "You big bull goanna, drop that!" The broody hen from whose clutch Gus had snatched the chicken was making a fearful fuss. She stood in front of her nest with her wings spread low to the ground, her comb bloodred, and her beak open, shrieking and dashing about in a frenzy. The other roosters, fowls, and turkeys were adding a deafening racket of cackles, clucks, and gobbles. The pigs in the nearby pens dashed off with a series of explosive snorts; the cows came running up with high alarm in their eyes; and the guinea fowls, which Mrs. Pine kept as sentries against foxes, set their clatter going like grinding stone crushers, loud enough to frighten every fox between Summertown and Gumbowie.

Without thinking, Burp rode Ginger around to the front of the sheds to investigate too. Just as he did so, a couple of white pullets, terrified by the din, dashed out between Ginger's legs. She reared up like a catapult and sprang back on her hind legs. The movement was too quick and violent for Burp, and he came down out of the saddle with a thud. Happily Ginger didn't bolt away, and Turps was able to leap across and grab her bridle. "You all right, Burp?" she asked quickly.

Burp got up grimacing and holding the seat of his pants. "Yeah! Just jarred my bones a bit."

"Whoa! Whoa, Ginger! There, girl! Everything's all right." Within a second or two Turps had the pony quiet again.

Meanwhile Gus had backed menacingly into a corner, the chicken, still held in his jaws, cheeping pitifully, and the hen flying defiantly at him in angry darts and rushes. Gus was an enormous goanna. He rose angrily on his claws, muscles tense and eyes flashing, looking for a way out of the trap he seemed to have drawn around himself.

"Look out!" Resin warned. "He can turn very nasty."

"Save the chick! Save the chick!" Columbine yelled.

"Fancy him going right inside the shed," Burp called, coming up. "He must've been pretty hungry."

"He's kind of tame. We've never frightened him before."

"Mum always suspects him, though," Turps said. "She reckons he often steals eggs and that."

38

"What are you going to do?"

Resin looked about him. "Get a stick or a pole or something. See if I can make him drop the chicken."

"Look out he doesn't go for you."

But Gus seemed as distrustful of them as they were of him. As soon as Resin moved away from the doorway, Gus made a dash for freedom, and the next moment he was racing across the yard like a low-flying arrow.

"Look out!"

"He's off!"

"There he goes!"

"After him!"

"Make him drop the chicken!"

They all joined in the chase. Woppit, Snap, and Blue, who had come down from the house, flew at Gus, barking and straining as he made his escape. The children followed in a straggling line, and Mr. and Mrs. Pine dropped what they were doing and ran to discover the cause of the uproar.

They were all running across the yard, shouting and calling, when there was a gallop of hooves behind them and Turps shot past on Ginger. She had swung herself into the saddle as soon as Gus had fled, and now, apart from Woppit, she was the only one with any chance of catching up with him. She leaped over the low railing fence by the gate and galloped off across the paddock.

"Look out he doesn't turn on you," Mr. Pine called. He stood with Mrs. Pine, Resin, Burp, and Columbine, watching from the fence. "They can get quite vicious," he said. "I can just imagine what sort of capers Ginger would get up to if that goanna suddenly jumped on her and hung on to her rump."

Perhaps it was just as well, therefore, that Ginger

didn't catch him. However, the thunder of her hooves and the eager barking of Woppit a few yards from Gus' tail did have some effect. Halfway across the paddock Gus dropped the chicken he had stolen, and then swept off toward the trees of The Big Scrub, narrowly beating Woppit to the first old gum tree. Turps turned and trotted back to pick up the chicken, but by now it was at its last gasp. She took it back to the others.

"Long, sneak-nosed thief," Mrs. Pine said sharply. "I hope this is a lesson to him."

Columbine pouted. "Poor Gus. He'll be so scared, he won't come back to the house for ages."

"Poor Gus, fiddlesticks. If he knows what's good for him, he won't come back to the house at all."

"Anyway," Mr. Pine said jovially, "Ginger has done something very few other horses have ever tried."

"Tossing Burp, for instance," Resin smirked.

"No, chasing goannas. And she made a jolly good job of it."

They all laughed then and went in to afternoon tea. All except Turps. She led Ginger back to the stable to brush her down. For Ginger came first—even before afternoon tea.

Pinch the Possum

When the September holidays started, Resin, Turps, and Columbine spent most of their time in The Big Scrub with Don and Debby Dobson. Some days they met Burp too, and the six of them went exploring. There were hundreds of things to find: hawks' eggs in high hollows, rabbit kittens in new burrows, neat miners' nests of horsehair, and magpies' nests of sprawling sticks, finches and tomtits in the bushes by the creek, tadpoles and baby frogs as quick as wet jelly in the pools, wild flowers and wattle and gum-tree blossoms on the slopes, and sometimes a great swirl of white feathers where one of Mrs. Pine's fowls had just been turned into a fox's breakfast.

One day when they were crossing the road to their front gate, Resin suddenly stopped and said, "Look."

Turps gave a start. "What?"

Resin ran over to a furry heap in the grass by the side of the road. His sister saw it then.

"What is it?"

"It's a possum. Been hit by a car."

Columbine looked at it, his mouth half open and his eyes agog. "Is . . . is it dead?"

Resin lifted it up gently. It lolled about, as limp as a rag.

"I think it is. Just dead. It's still warm."

Then he gave an excited shout. "Turps, look, there's a baby in her pouch, see?"

It was true. The baby was so small that it lay in the palm of Resin's hand like a curled-up mouse. Columbine crowded forward to see.

"Gee, Turps, it's weeny. Is it alive?"

"Yes, it's still living, but it'll die without its mother."

Turps turned quickly to her big brother. "Do you think we could save it? Do you think we could?"

"We can try. Come on!" And they ran up to the house in a flurry of legs and yells.

That was how the long story of the possum started. For days they thought of nothing else. They fed it with milk from an eyedropper, a drip at a time. They wrapped it in an old woolen scarf and put it by the fire. They tiptoed over to it a hundred times a day to see if its eyes were open or closed; and they felt its tiny sides to see if it was still breathing. Once Mum almost trod on it, and twice they caught Puss'll-do, his eyes narrow with suspicion and malice, sniffing at the woolen bundle. Sometimes they came close to cooking it when the fire flared up, and sometimes they found it half frozen when it wriggled out of its scarf. But after a week of panic and suspense they saved it.

Soon it began to grow quickly; it scrabbled about the palms of their hands, fossicked until it found a finger or a thumb, and then, clamping its little jaws on it as firmly as it could, bit with all its strength. Luckily it wasn't strong enough to break the skin, but there was no doubt about what it wanted to do. Turps yelled as the tiny teeth needled her hand and left a couple of sharp pink dents. "Ouch! Ouch! You little brute. You can pinch like nippers already." And from that moment he was christened "Pinch the Possum."

Luckily he grew tamer and tamer, so that by the time he was big enough to really sink his teeth into somebody's hand and cover the place in blood, he no longer wanted to do it. Sometimes he jumped on Mr. Pine's lap and grabbed his wrist or cheek, or the lobe of his ear, as if about to bite it through. But then he just pinched it playfully or kissed it with his tongue like a parrot before skittering off across the room.

By the time he was half grown, Pinch knew the run of the house. Mum was very strict about it, though, and would only allow him to have a romp inside for half an hour each evening, when the children came home from school. For the rest of the time he had to be locked up in an old fowl shed down in the yard.

Mr. Pine agreed with their mother. "No," he said firmly, "we have enough trouble with possums as it is, in the fruit trees and the sheds, in the feed bins, and on the roofs at night. Keep Pinch locked up."

Turps looked at her father shrewdly. "It's illegal to keep possums locked up," she said; "they're protected." But her father was hard. "Good!" he answered. "Then take him out into The Big Scrub and turn him loose."

"Ah, gee, Dad! Gosh!"

And so Pinch stayed in his shed all day, sleeping in a hollow log and waking up just before tea to have a romp

43

with the family. He loped up the passage in a swaggering sort of way, sniffing with his keen, thin nose like an anteater, and springing as lightly as a gibbon from chair to chair, leaping onto the mantelshelf, curtains, and pelmets, or fleeing suddenly like a gray blur into the bedroom.

He was perfectly happy to sniff and explore silently through the house, as long as there were no noises or interruptions. But the moment a door banged, or footsteps sounded, he was gone.

As often as not he fled to one of his friends for protection. Even a tiny movement was enough to set him off— a shoe shifted, a newspaper rustled, or an itch scratched. Sometimes they didn't even know what had caused it. They only knew that something gray had swept through the air like a shadow and landed, plop, on their legs or thighs. A second later it had whipped up their sides, and something quick and soft and furry was balancing on their heads, with a couple of sharp little forearms clawing at an ear or a collar for support.

Then they would put up their hands and tickle him under his belly and say, "Hullo, Pinch! What are you scared about this time? Come on down." And they would lift him down gently and put him on the floor again till the next time.

Mr. Pine and Resin usually wore overalls or long trousers, so they didn't mind Pinch's claws racing about on them. But Turps and her mother weren't so lucky, unless they were wearing slacks.

But the biggest upheaval happened when Aunt Hester and Uncle Stan paid them a visit. They lived in Summertown, about thirty miles away, and they loved to come out to the farm, as they said.

Aunt Hester was a telephone post of a woman, with a

tall thin body, and cheeks as hard and smooth as porcelain insulators. And she was a great talker.

"Worse than an automatic exchange," Mr. Pine said. *"Natter, natter, clack, clack, clack.* Continuous service. She never hangs up."

To make matters worse she moved in quick jerky darts, her arms going like signals. It was no wonder that Pinch took fright. He came loping into the kitchen so silently that no one even saw him sitting there on his haunches by the saucepan cupboard, just as Aunt Hester was describing her adventure with a nasty door-to-door salesman.

She told her story excitingly. "So I walked right up to him," she said, "and then I suddenly pointed my finger straight at his face, like this, and I said: *Eeeeeeeeeeeeek!"* Mrs. Pine spilled the milk, and Turps and Columbine jumped with fright. For Aunt Hester, who had made a quick jab with her arm to show how she had pointed at the man, suddenly doubled up and clapped her hands to her leg. And there she stood, shrieking, "Eeeeeeeeeeeeek, Eeeeeeeeeeeeek," at the top of her voice, and grabbing at a squirming bundle she had trapped with her dress just above her knee.

Mrs. Pine rushed over to grab at the bundle too, and Aunt Hester changed her cry from "Eeeeeeeeek!" to "Ooooooooooooh!"

"Don't pull at him," Resin yelled as he jumped forward; "he'll dig in."

"Ahhoooooooooh."

It was too late. Aunt Hester had given the bundle a hard tug, and four sets of claws had ripped her leg like fishhooks.

Turps ran forward too.

"Let me," she said.

"Aaaaahooooh," Aunt Hester wailed, still tugging and yelling.

"*Don't pull*, Aunty."

But Aunt Hester gave another desperate shriek and grabbed at the bundle under her dress so hard that she almost crushed it. The bundle gave a violent jerk and started to move.

"Eeeeeeeek! It's climbing higher."

Turps was on her knees beside her aunt.

"Stand still, Aunty. I'll get him."

"Ooooooh! Ooooooh!"

"Shhhhh! Quiet, Aunty."

Slowly and carefully Turps reached up and unhooked Pinch's claws one by one from Aunt Hester's leg, and lifted him down.

"Oh, poor Pinch," she said, cuddling him. "Did the poor little fellow get a bad fright?"

Aunt Hester's face was as red as a stoplight.

"Poor fellow!" she cried in disgust. "A bad fright! What about *me*?" And gathering cotton wool, antiseptic, ointment, and sticking plaster from Mrs. Pine, she swept off into the bathroom and slammed the door shut behind her, crying, "Monster! Monster!" all the way down the corridor.

Mrs. Pine was very stern. "Really, Crystal," she said. "I thought you had more sense."

Turps pretended to be crestfallen. She knew that whenever her mother drew herself up and called her "Crystal" instead of "Turps," she was doing it mainly for effect and didn't really believe it herself.

"Bringing that creature inside when we have visitors," her mother was saying. "Half-wild brute that it is."

Turps looked up archly. Out of the corner of her eye

she caught sight of Resin, standing with his hands in his pockets and a smirk on his face.

"Go on. Take him back to his cage this minute." But a faint smile seemed to be flickering around the corners of her mouth. Just then Uncle Stan and Dad came hurrying in from outside, asking what all the commotion was about. When Uncle Stan heard what had happened, he laughed until his sides ached.

"Wooden legs or armor plate," he said, wiping his eyes. "That's what you need when you visit the Pines. I must warn everyone in Summertown." And he laughed again till everyone else joined in. Everyone except Aunt Hester. She was still simmering about the face like a pot of tomato soup. And so, as soon as Uncle Stan and Dad heard the bathroom door opening, they suddenly looked very serious and started to talk about the weather.

The spotlight hunt

It was a week after Aunt Hester's disastrous visit. Columbine had been sent to bed early because this time *he* was in disgrace. That afternoon he had driven the tractor through two fences, a gate, and the cowyard sliprails before his father had been able to leap on board and save him and the rest of the farm from destruction. It had all happened in the minute or two after Mr. Pine had left the tractor at the back gate with the engine running and hurried inside to make a telephone call. While he was away, Columbine had climbed into the driver's seat to impress Debby Dobson and, manipulating all the levers and pedals he could find, had accidentally set the tractor in motion. A brief rampage through gates and fences followed, with Columbine, white-faced, hanging desperately on to the steering wheel, and Debby Dobson shrieking the alarm through the neighborhood.

Luckily Resin was not in the yard at the time, and

so he had escaped implication in the crime. This was particularly important just now because, after months of begging, he and Burp Heaslip had been told that they could go with the men on a spotlight-shooting trip that night, and it would have been unbearable if the privilege had been withdrawn at the last minute.

They had wanted to go on such a trip for years, but the answer had always been "too dangerous for boys," or "wait till you grow up." But at last Mr. Pine and Mr. Heaslip had relented. The boys could come, provided they sat in the cabin and did exactly as they were told. And so, while Columbine, tearful and sniveling, clutched his pillow, Resin set off in the truck with his father on a great fox hunt.

The party met at Heaslips' at eight o'clock. There were seven of them altogether—Mr. Pine in the driver's cabin, with Resin and Burp; Mr. Heaslip, Mr. Dobson, and Emil Eckert on the tray of the truck with their guns and ammunition; and Burp's big brother Harold working the spotlight. The back of the truck looked like an arsenal: Mr. Heaslip and Mr. Dobson each had a nine-shot automatic rifle, and Emil climbed on board carrying two rifles and a ponderous double-barreled shotgun. Buckled across his chest from his right shoulder was an old bandolier that looked as if it had been used by the German army in 1871. It was loaded down with dozens of cartridges, their new caps glinting in the light like brass buttons.

"Well, Ben," he said to Mr. Heaslip, "dis time we give dem beggars somet'ing to t'ink about, eh?" He laughed a laugh that sounded like a trundling barrel. Mr. Heaslip laughed too. He was a jovial, round-faced man, a grown-up version of Burp. His name was Ben, or Beneaslip to everyone else.

They had organized a hunt because the foxes were especially bad just then. Every night they came out of The Big Scrub to raid poultry runs and chicken coops. Fowls, ducks, roosters, turkeys, geese, even spring lambs —all seemed to be fair game to a hungry vixen with hungry cubs. But it wasn't just what they stole and ate that angered the farmers; it was the senseless slaughter of poultry that the foxes had no intention of eating. One night Emil's wife lost twenty-three big turkeys—and the next morning found twenty-one of them lying scattered about the paddock with their heads bitten off and their throats torn open, but with the flesh untouched.

"By yiminy," old Emil vowed, "no fox better not get friendly wit' me tonight. He better watch his tail."

"You'll put salt on it, eh?" asked Beneaslip.

"Hoch! Pretty heavy salt it will be!"

The three shooters strapped themselves firmly in place. On the back of the truck a row of upright sheep hurdles had been put securely around the edge of the tray. They were about three feet six inches high, made of wood and steel, and just the right height to give balance and support to a man standing with a gun in his hands. George Dobson and Beneaslip stood on one side, and Emil, who was a crack shot, on the other. Each one buckled a broad leather strap around one of the uprights and ran the belt around his waist, something like a telephone linesman working on a pole. For there were certain things they had to be thorough and careful about. Spotlight shooting could be very dangerous, and there had been some terrible accidents when guns had gone off accidentally or shooters had lost their balance on a swerving truck just as they were about to fire.

It was therefore arranged that Mr. Dobson and Ben-easlip would shoot from one side and Emil from the other; they would never cross their fire and they would never shoot at anything they couldn't see clearly. Harold Heaslip's job was to swivel the spotlight from the top of the cabin and, once he had picked out a fox in its beam, never to let it escape.

At last everything was ready and they set off, rumbling down the track from the Heaslips' house until they came to the open paddocks. There Resin's father cruised up and down in a set pattern while Harold swept the night with the beam like a searchlight. At first they didn't have much luck. A few rabbits, an old tomcat, a possum or two feeding near the gum trees by the creek—each came into the beam in turn, but the hunters didn't even raise their guns. They were searching for bigger quarry tonight.

Mr. Pine put his head out of the truck window and called back to the others. "We'll cross the road into my block; we might find the blighters nearer to The Big Scrub."

"Okay."

"And den down on mine blace too," Emil called. "By golly dere is more foxes down dere dan stems of grass."

The truck bumped across the road, swung through the open gates of Bottlebrush Barn, and pulled into the pasture paddock next to The Big Scrub. Resin and Burp sat forward eagerly on the cabin seat, peering out through the windshield.

"Gosh, I hope it isn't a washout," Resin said uneasily. "We must've been driving about for half an hour, I reckon."

"Easy," Burp agreed.

They bumped on in silence. "D'you ever have a wash-out, Dad?" Resin asked.

"Not often. We usually see at least a couple, sometimes a dozen or more."

"D'you always get the ones you see?"

"I wish we did." Mr. Pine laughed sourly. "Some are out of range; some are just the glint of an eye in the dark or a second's silhouette; some get back into The Big Scrub before we can have a decent go at them."

"And you can't follow them there."

"Not without a helicopter."

They rode on again, lulled by the warm hum of the engine.

"There!"

"Offside."

Crack! A rifle shot rattled right in Resin's ear, it seemed so close. Boom! Boom! The twin roar of Emil's enormous shotgun reverberated through the cabin like an earthquake.

"Got 'em! Good shot, Emil."

"Hoch! Dat put saltpeter on d' tails, eh?" Emil was jovially reloading his artillery piece. "How you like dat?" he called to the dead foxes. "Tit for tat, eh! Dat's for Emma's twenty-one turkeys, you t'ieving beggars."

Down in the cabin Resin and Burp were beside themselves with frustration and curiosity. For they hadn't seen a thing. The warning shout by Harold, the hard dart of his spotlight like a probe of frozen white fire, the reports of the guns—it had all happened in seconds. It wasn't until now, when the truck pulled up and the light focused on the two bodies in turn, that they saw the foxes for the first time.

"D'you want the skins, Harry?" Beneaslip called.

"I'll toss them onto the truck if you like," Harold said, preparing to leap down.

"We'll get them," Resin and Burp yelled together, flinging open the cabin door and tumbling out.

"Stay where you are!" It was such a roar that they both stood stock-still. "Get back into the truck, you idiots."

They climbed back shamefacedly, especially Resin, who had never heard his father use such a tone before.

"But . . . "

"Don't you ever jump from a spotlighting truck again!" Mr. Pine was so furious that they could see the anger in his eyes by the light of the dashboard.

"You don't ever leave this cabin till I say so. Understand?"

"Yes, Dad!"

"Those chaps up there are pretty light on the trigger, especially old Emil. You rush out from the truck like that in the dark and they're just as likely to take you for a fox or a kangaroo and put a bullet through you before anyone's got time to think."

"Yes, Dad."

"So sit tight, and don't wriggle an eyebrow till I tell you to."

"Yes, Dad."

Harold had collected the two dead foxes and was holding them up in front of the headlights of the truck. "Skins aren't worth a cracker," he called. "Emil's made a sieve out of 'em with that great blunderbuss of his."

"All right, don't bother then."

Harold climbed back on board and manned the spotlight again.

"It was a male und a female," Emil said, "a fox and a

53

vixen. Dat is good; dey won't no more cubs be breeding, eh?"

The truck set off again, cruising systematically up and down the paddock.

"How did they get two foxes so close together?" Resin asked.

"A pair," Mr. Pine said tersely. "Probably mating."

"I didn't even see them."

"They were on the offside. Usually they break up before we can get at them, but Old Emil must have been too quick for 'em."

They cruised on steadily.

"There!" It was Harold's warning cry again.

This time Resin and Burp saw it too—the bright coals of the fox's eyes in the spotlight—but they were still a long way off. Mr. Pine stamped on the accelerator and hurtled down at breakneck speed to take him by surprise. But the fox was a wily old fellow. He slipped into a steep creek bed out of sight, doubled back quickly, and escaped into the scrub before they could pick him up again. Nobody fired a shot.

"Never mind," Emil called. "Two for us, and one for dem."

After combing the open paddocks at Bottlebrush Barn without sighting anything else, they switched over to the Dobsons' farm and shot three more within half an hour. Back on Beneaslip's they killed another one, and finally set off for Emil's property three or four miles down the Gumbowie road.

"All I hope is dat tonight dey come down by Emma's fowl shed again to catch more turkey gobblers," Emil said.

"You'll give them the drumstick, eh, Emil?" Mr. Dobson said.

"D' double drumstick," Emil answered emphatically. "Right in d' eyes between."

He could hardly have wished more successfully. As soon as they turned into his farm the chase began. There seemed to be foxes everywhere. They saw five in the first paddock by the house, but only managed to get two of them. They flushed another one from an alfalfa patch near the dam, and then drove up into Emil's far paddock near the Range. Here they soon lost count. To Resin and Burp it sounded as if a cannonade was coming from the back of the truck, mingled with Harold's shouts of "There! There!" and Emil's triumphant whoops. "By yiminy," he bellowed after a particularly furious bombardment, "dese barrels is getting too hot to touch mit d' fingers, nearly."

Inside the cabin Resin and Burp were almost bursting through the windshield. "There's one," they'd yell as the headlights picked up the glowing eyes or the fleeing target of back or brush. "There's another one! Look! Look!"

Mr. Pine performed astounding feats at the wheel of the truck, executing maneuvers that no racing driver had ever heard of. Back on the tray, the four men lurched and swung, feet planted wide apart, safety belts as taut as hawsers, guns smoking in their hands.

"That ought to clean your place up a bit," George Dobson said when the fury died down at last.

Emil wiped the great ham of his hand across his face and left it streaked with burnt gunpowder.

"By yiminy, I t'ink so too," he said.

"We got more than half of them," Beneaslip put in,

"and the rest ought to get the message that they're not too popular around here."

Resin's father leaned out of the truck window. "Time to make tracks for home?" he asked.

"About time."

"We'll drop in at my place and have a cup of tea."

"Good."

They set off across the paddock but they'd gone less than a quarter of a mile when Harold's yell echoed through the night again. "There! There!" The spotlight beam pointed clear and sharp; the shooters grabbed their guns again; and Mr. Pine trod down the accelerator.

It was a big fox, the biggest for the night. He was caught out in the open, far from shelter, but he was fresh and he was going like a missile. A rifle cracked but the shot went wide.

"Wait!" yelled Emil. "Too far. Range is too far." He shouted to Mr. Pine. "Go to it, 'Arry. Catch dis fellow up if you can. He is big as a dingo. I t'ink he is d' one dat finished up all Emma's turkeys."

Mr. Pine was gaining, and they knew that the fox knew it too.

"Look out," Beneaslip yelled. "He'll double back in a minute."

He was right. The fox, sensing that his pursuers were coming up behind him, suddenly stopped short and turned; as the truck hurtled past him, he darted across behind it and made off at right angles to the way he'd been going. He was making for the nearest part of The Scrub, but he still had over half a mile to go.

Resin's father spun the wheel and the truck lurched around. Mr. Dobson and Beneaslip both fired but they were off-balance and missed. Emil was on the wrong side and couldn't use his gun. Harold lost sight of the fox for a second or two, and by the time he'd picked him up in the spotlight again, they had lost sixty or seventy yards.

"There! There!"

"Step on him, 'Arry," yelled Emil, meaning the accelerator, not the fox. "Or he will into d' Scrub be getting."

Mr. Pine drove like a demon, but it took a while for the truck to gather speed and gain ground again.

"Now!"

But the fox stopped short again just as Emil fired. The blast went over his head, the truck careered past him again, and by the time they'd swung around, he had repeated his maneuver, doubled around behind the truck, and was racing ahead again toward the safety of The Scrub.

"*Donnerwetter!*" thundered Emil, yanking out another cartridge from his bandolier and slapping it into the smoking breech. "Dis fellow is getting too smart, eh?"

"There he is!"

Resin and Burp both yelled as the spotlight picked him up again. He was to the right of the truck, well ahead and running strongly. Mr. Dobson and Beneaslip took careful aim and fired; the two automatic rifles sounded like a machine gun. One, two, three, four, five—the boys could see the dirt kicking up at the fox's feet where the bullets thudded into the ground, but every one of them missed. Empty shells rattled on the cabin and bounced down in front of the windshield.

"Thunderation!" Beneaslip had to stop to reload.

"Step on him, 'Arry," shouted Emil, "or he vill be getting away from us yet."

The truck rocketed along and for the third time they began to draw up to the fox. They all knew that this would be their last chance because The Scrub was only a hundred yards away.

"Dis time, den!" Emil took deliberate aim.

"Look out!"

"Hang on!"

"Verdammt!"

A washout three feet deep suddenly loomed up in the beam of the headlights—as jagged and sharp as an earthquake fissure. There was a screech of brakes and the truck broadsided on two wheels in a cloud of dust. Harold was flung on his back on the floor of the truck and the three shooters were hurled about in their safety belts like rag puppets. In the cabin Resin and Burp heard the double crash of Emil's shotgun before everything skidded dizzily in front of their eyes. For a second they thought the whole truck was going to turn over, but it righted itself at the last minute and spun around facing the direction it had come from. As it did so, the passengers' door flew open and Resin went somersaulting into Emil's paddock.

"Melton!"

Even as he thumped the ground with a thud that jarred his bones he heard his father's cry. He didn't remember anything else very clearly. He got up rather dizzily as the truck skidded to a stop, and everyone leaped out and ran to him.

"Melton! Are you all right?"

Resin remembered trying to laugh weakly. "Yeah! Good . . . good as gold."

"For God's sake, boy, you could have been killed!"

"Why did d' door come open?"

Resin guessed why. He'd been holding on to the handle during the furious chase after the fox, and when he'd

58

been flung against the door he'd accidentally pressed it down with the weight of his body. But he was too dazed and shamefaced to admit it.

The men walked back a little way, looking at the skid marks. "By yiminy," Emil said, "we was nearly up d' creek dat time, 'Arry."

"I wish you'd warn me about your tank traps next time," Mr. Pine said testily. "What d'you think would have happened to my truck if I'd hit that at fifty?"

"Would make a mess."

"A mess? It could have killed the lot of us—all for the sake of a little fox."

"A big fox, very big fox," Emil corrected.

"Yes, but he's still not worth a truck."

"And he got away," Emil added with chagrin. "Now I t'ink he vill more turkeys be vanting for Christmas, eh?"

"Yes, you'll have to wait till next year to get him now," Beneaslip said, taking out his pipe. "It's too late this year."

He was right. After October the risk of fire was too great to allow spotlight shooters open entry into the paddocks. A smoldering wad from a cartridge falling into dry grass could start a bushfire and wipe out the whole district—a high price to pay for a fox or a rabbit.

"Time we were home," Resin's father said. "All aboard."

Resin climbed gratefully into the cabin again and lolled his head against the back of the seat. He suddenly felt very tired and dizzy. His eyes began to close in the warmth of the cabin and he had a strange half-dream of foxes with burning tails, running about with shotguns in their hands and setting fire to his father's crops.

Strarvy and Lemon

The possum had really done Aunt Hester more harm than the children thought. It wasn't just that her leg had long claw scratches from the thigh to the knee; it was the suspicion and unbelief on other people's faces, when she told them the story, that annoyed her more than anything.

"How did you get those dreadful scratches on your leg?" everyone would ask when she bounced out scrawnily onto the Saturday-afternoon tennis courts at Summertown.

"Oh, a possum ran up my leg . . . " she would begin.

Then it came—the raised eyebrows, the heads turned away, and the smirks and titters on the sides of their faces. Aunt Hester would go home furious.

"They just won't believe me, Stanley," she would shout at poor Uncle Stan. "That creature of Muriel's has made me the laughingstock of the town."

60

"It isn't Muriel's, dear. It belongs to the children. And it's not a monster—just a quick, mischievous possum. Quite a pet really."

Aunt Hester pigeoned out her chest in disgust. "Pet! I'll pet him! If I ever get him alone again, I'll ring his neck."

Luckily the children didn't hear about all this.

Mr. and Mrs. Pine didn't often go up to Summertown. They did most of their shopping at Barnacle's store, or at the shops at Upper Gumbowie, and the school bus helped to supply them too. Moreover, there were important things going on around them that helped to occupy the children's attention and temporarily made them forget the angry antics of their aunt.

For Strarvy and Lemon were behaving very strangely. Turps mentioned it at the tea table one Friday night. She was always the first to notice such things.

"Miss Lemmen came home in the bus again tonight," she remarked, looking at no one in particular.

"Oh," Mrs. Pine said noncommittally.

"She stayed at the Dobsons' house over the weekend," Resin joined in, "so that she could be near Strarvy."

"That's the third time in a month," Turps put in. "And the fourth one was the long weekend. That time *he* went to stay in Gumbowie with her."

"What's she want to be near him for?" young Columbine asked, munching his apple noisily.

"Near him is right," Turps said, tossing her curls. "She just about sits on his lap in the bus."

"Yes, but what for?" Columbine asked, munching his apple and fixing his sister with a keen, wide look.

But his mother interrupted them firmly. "That's enough, Colin," she said. "What Mr. Harvey and Miss

61

Lemmen do in their spare time is none of our business. And how often have I told you not to speak with your mouth full?" she added abruptly. "For goodness' sake, learn some manners."

But Columbine wasn't going to be fooled. He knew that Strarvy and Lemon were up to something, and that his mother and sister were trying to keep it from him. So he decided to watch them more carefully than ever.

He didn't have long to wait. The next day was Saturday, and the usual weekend jobs were waiting to be done. After the cows had been milked, and the fowls, pigs, calves, and pets had all been fed, Resin went down to clean the sheds, and Turps helped her mother bake the weekly supply of cakes, scones, and biscuits.

Columbine had to make a hard choice. He was torn between going with his brother, and perhaps being lucky enough to turn up a nest of young mice, or staying with his sister and knowing for certain that he would have spoons to lick, the mixture to taste, and the broken biscuits to eat. He decided in favor of the kitchen.

It was a lucky choice. They had barely finished cutting out the last batch when suddenly Mrs. Pine looked up at the clock.

"A quarter to eleven," she said hastily. "Goodness, and I wanted to go down to the shop before lunch."

"I'll go," Columbine said instantly.

"Good, you can get me some jelly crystals and matches."

"That's all?"

"Oh, and . . . " His mother paused. "No, I'll have to come with you after all. Your school shoes are worn right through at the toes. We'll have to see if Old Barnacle has a pair that'll fit."

"Oh, goody."

"Never mind goodying. Brush your old ones and come on down."

It was less than ten minutes to Old Barnacle's store. When they arrived there were two other people, a man and a woman, standing side by side at the counter, with their backs to the door and their shoulders touching. In the dim light it was hard to see very clearly, but Columbine had the impression that it was unnecessary for two people to stand so closely together when there was such a lot of space to spare on either side of them.

"Aren't you afraid someone will open up a big shopping center or supermarket here?" the man was saying.

Barnacle laughed. It was one of his hard, scornful laughs that jingled the post-office scales and set the sausages swinging above their heads.

"Here? On this sleepy old cow track? They wouldn't look at the place; and if they did, the dust would smother everything in a day, like cinnamon or pepper."

"Yes, I guess it would."

"No guessing. When you've been here for forty years like me, you know."

"No doubt."

"They wouldn't even build a supermarket in Gumbowie. Summertown would be the nearest. That's thirty miles away."

"Yes."

"And in any case," Barnacle said, drawing himself up into an enormous mountain, "they'd be scared."

"Scared?"

"Scared of me. Of the competition. I stock everything. Always have."

He brought the huge flat slap of his palm down on

the counter as he always did when he wanted to stress something very loudly.

"Every blessed thing."

There was something about the two people Barnacle was talking to that interested Columbine, but it wasn't until they turned to go that he suddenly saw why. He knew them. They were Strarvy and Lemon.

"Hullo, Colin."

"Hullo, Miss Strarvy and Miss Lemon."

"Good morning, Mrs. Pine."

"Good morning, Miss Lemmen, Mr. Harvey."

It all seemed a babble of names to Columbine before they finally got down to doing any talking. But his mother soon made up for that.

"Doing some shopping?"

"Not much really. A few things for Mrs. Dobson."

"Did you walk?"

"Yes."

"Lovely morning for a walk."

"Beautiful."

"Would you like some morning tea before you go back?"

Lemon looked quickly up at Strarvy before she answered Columbine's mother. "It's very kind of you, Mrs. Pine, but . . ."

"Hot scones. Crystal has only just taken them out of the oven."

"With jam and cream," Columbine piped in.

Strarvy laughed heartily. "Not baked in the oven with jam and cream surely?"

"No. Afterward."

They were all laughing.

"We'd love to come," Strarvy said. "It's on our way,

and we can take the shortcut through The Big Scrub afterward."

"Good. Now I'll just get some shoes for Colin and we'll all go back together."

Strarvy and Lemon were in a wonderfully good mood that day. In Mrs. Pine's kitchen they sat at the table together, laughing and munching in turns, and constantly glancing at one another. Strarvy was more than usually talkative, and Lemon's face for once was shiny and pink with a blossoming kind of half blush. Turps kept offering them more scones and cakes and tea. And then Columbine, who had been puzzling over the mystery for a long time, made a tremendous discovery.

He accidentally dropped half a scone, and dived down to snatch it off the floor before Puss'll-do could get it. Down there he had a strange beetle's-eye view of the world—a world of shoes and legs and knees and unswept bits on the floor.

And then he saw hands. There were two of them, and they didn't belong to the same person. One was a man's hand and one was a woman's, and they were knotting themselves about and clasping each other very firmly. Down beneath the table Columbine nearly called out with excitement. Strarvy and Lemon were holding hands under the tablecloth!

It was the kind of news that Columbine couldn't possibly keep to himself. He knew better than to blurt it out in front of their guests, but it was a discovery that stirred and astonished him so much he could hardly wait for Strarvy and Lemon to say good-bye. And as soon as they had gone, he shouted it out. But to his disappointment neither Turps nor his mother seemed surprised.

"But what did they want to *do* that for?" he demanded.

"They're . . . well, I guess they are going to announce their engagement," Turps said at last.

"Announce their *what*?" Columbine asked, screwing up his face in distaste and bewilderment.

"Their engagement."

"What's that?"

"It means that they are probably going to get married," said his mother clearly, "but we don't know for sure yet."

"Why don't you know? They were holding hands."

"Yes, but well . . . that doesn't mean they are going to for certain."

"And they were giggling and all that."

"But they haven't announced it yet in the paper."

"Aren't they sure yet?"

"Probably, but they haven't said it out aloud yet to other people."

"Why not?"

"Oh, for goodness' sake, Columbine." Turps turned on him angrily and started to clear the table.

Columbine knew that this source of information had dried up, so he skipped out onto the veranda and ran down to the yard.

Strarvy and Lemon were just disappearing up the track that ran through part of The Big Scrub where it came down like a snout between the paddocks of the Dobsons and the Pines.

As he saw them go, walking more and more slowly, shoulder pressed against shoulder, Columbine had a mischievous inspiration. If he followed them carefully for a while, perhaps he would hear them say it out aloud. They certainly *looked* as though they were ready. And then he really would have stolen a march on Turps.

He ran up the track to the bend where they'd disappeared, his feet plopping softly in the thick dust. There
they were, only a chain or two ahead. Strarvy had his
arm around Lemon now, and they were walking very
slowly indeed. Sometimes Columbine thought they would
stop altogether, but each time they managed to keep
their feet moving.

The track twisted and turned constantly through the
bush, so he kept losing sight of them. But all he had to
do was to move silently to the next bend, and there they
were again. And because they never looked back, it was
the easiest job of tracking that anyone could have had.
That was why Columbine was all the more bewildered
when, coming casually up to the fifth or sixth bend, he
suddenly found they had disappeared. He ran silently on
to the next curve. Still no sign of them. Columbine's heart
beat with excitement and exhaustion.

They had obviously left the track to look for a little
hidden spot where they could announce whatever it was.
He listened tensely. Above the beat of his own pulse, he
imagined he heard sounds. Voices, perhaps, in very low
tones. Though his father and mother had told him a
thousand times that he must *never* go into The Big Scrub
on his own, he stepped cautiously off the track, climbed
over a fallen log, and paused. Ahead of him the ground
dipped down toward a small creek bed, with big gums
and smaller growth jostling more thickly than ever. And
from somewhere among them came the sounds he had
heard.

He listened again, curious and afraid. They were
voices. Young voices. He ventured a few steps farther,
went around the butt of an old stump, and stopped,

astonished. In a clear patch between the trees sat Resin and Donny Dobson, side by side, like two old swagmen, smoking pipes!

For a minute Columbine was too surprised to call out. Then he ran forward.

"Hey, Resin," he yelled. At the same time, he tripped over a stick, and sprawled almost in Donny's lap.

His sudden appearance had a shattering effect on the two smokers. They had been sitting there so calmly and complacently, drawing at the pipe stems until the tobacco in the bowls glowed like gentle volcanoes, that they might have been a couple of old philosophers or drovers yarning in the sun. But now they sprang apart wildly. Donny's pipe was knocked from his hand and the hot coals and ashes went flying everywhere.

"Whoooo!" Donny yelled, as if the wind had just been knocked out of him.

"Ouch," cried Resin, snatching his pipe from his mouth and burning his fingers as he tried to hide it behind his back.

"Look out, mind the . . . Columbine!"

There was such a mixture of relief and exasperation in Donny's voice that Resin almost laughed out loud.

"What the heck are *you* doing here? Gaw, you half frightened the tripe out of a bloke. I thought it was Dad or the cops for sure."

Resin wrinkled his nose and sniffed. "Hey something's burning. Donny, are you on fire?"

Donny searched about and brushed his clothes in an angry sort of way. "Gee, I hope not. I'll sure cop it if I burn a hole in my pants."

"Your stuff went everywhere. Flying sparks an' that."

"It wasn't me! It was Columbine, busting in."

68

"It's all under the grass. You can smell it smoking and stinking."

"Well, stamp on it then."

They started kicking and thumping at the grass, all three of them, thudding and stamping as if they were crushing the life out of an adder of fire. They were so busy searching and scratching about that they had no time to think of anything else. It wasn't until Resin began scouting around in a wider circle from the point of Donny's disaster, that he suddenly sighted something strange on the ground. It was a pair of shoes, men's shoes, with a pair of gray trousers standing above them. Beside them was a pair of ladies' shoes, with legs in them.

Resin stopped short, and his heart gave a thump.

"I should think so," a male voice above him said.

All three boys looked up quickly.

Strarvy and Lemon were standing by the butt of the big gum tree, looking down at them severely. Columbine gave a squeak of surprise and astonishment as Strarvy came a step forward.

"What in heaven's name do you think you're doing, you three? Trying to burn out the district?"

Donny and Columbine hung their heads, and Resin scuffed at the ground with his toe. Lemon came forward, too, and Columbine, who was in her class, fidgeted miserably.

"Were you smoking?"

"Of course they were smoking," said Strarvy in a blunt, gruff voice. "Playing with matches like big babies."

Resin suddenly remembered that he had his pipe in his hand, and he tried to hide it behind his back.

"Don't try to hide it, you poor ninny. Honestly, I thought you'd have had more sense."

69

Strarvy turned abruptly to Donny. "And where's yours, Sir Walter Raleigh?"

Donny looked about miserably. "I . . . I don't know, sir. It got knocked out of my hand."

"Well, *look*, boy! There it is, over by the log."

Donny hastily retrieved it, and stood there sheepishly.

"Now, listen, you three," Strarvy said, in his best schoolteacher's voice—the sort he always used when he was about to give someone a lecture. But he saw the look of resignation cloud the boys' faces and changed his mind.

"The first thing we have to do is check the grass and dead leaves, to make sure nothing is smoldering. I'm glad that at least you had the sense to start doing *that*."

They all searched and stamped about like horses, with Lemon's trim little whinny and prance joining in.

"You don't know how lucky you are," Strarvy said, panting and thudding his heels about. "What if this had happened a week or two later? What then?"

"Well," Resin began tentatively, "the grass around here was still a bit green and we thought because it was very calm and . . . "

"And because there were plenty of dead leaves about, and dry bark and twigs, and a good chance of a north wind coming up. How could you be so *stupid*!"

They all smarted under his scorn.

"Where did you get the pipes?"

"W-e-l-l." Donny cleared his throat rather painfully. "Actually they're Grandpa's. They were in his bureau."

"So you stole them?"

Donny protested inwardly against the word "stole." "I . . . I . . . just borrowed them."

"And Grandpa's tobacco?"

"Yes."

70

"And his matches?"

"No, they were from the kitchen."

"Give them to me."

"All . . . all of them?"

"Everything! Pipes, tobacco, matches—the lot."

"You . . . you won't tell Dad will you, sir? He- . . . he'd wallop the living daylights out of me."

For the first time Strarvy seemed to relent a little. "We'll see," he said. He collected Grandpa's smoking apparatus, took Lemon's arm, and turned to go back onto the track.

"And remember," he said severely over his shoulder, "it wasn't for want of trying that you didn't start the first big bushfire of the season today. You might have better luck next time."

And with that he and Lemon walked off through the trees and disappeared.

The Gumbowie Show

The Annual Gumbowie Show was always held in Upper
Gumbowie on a Saturday early in November. It was a big
show because the town was in a central position in the
district and had built up a fine reputation. Everyone came
crowding from distant farms and stations to compete, and
all kinds of sideshow men set up their booths and yelled
and coaxed and entreated the local people not to miss
their one and only chance of seeing the sensational Hairy
Man from the Zambezi, or Malgo the Magician who
could saw a woman in half and then put her together
again.

There were sheaf-tossing competitions for the strong
and skillful young farmers, and cake-baking competitions
for their wives; there were parades of cattle and horses,
prizes for pickles and embroidery, and booths touting
dried sausages and afternoon teas. There was a large
section for schoolwork and homecrafts, and a competition

for dolls and pets. And finally, as a sort of climax to the entertainment on the Town Oval, all the district Emergency Fire Service Units competed for an efficiency award, and a shield which the winners held for a year. They came hurtling onto the arena in their trucks immediately after a row of fires had suddenly burst out at one end of the ground, and then, in a furious moment of rivalry, they all tried to bring their equipment up and douse the fire in the shortest possible time. There was a great deal of cheering and shouted advice while all this was going on, but the teams took their work very seriously and proved that they were thoroughly efficient and well organized.

Bottlebrush Barn was a bustle of activity on the morning of the Show. Mr. Pine was loading two calves, a sow, and a litter of sucking piglets onto the truck; Turps was riding her pony Ginger over to the Dobsons', who were going to take her in with two of their own horses; Mrs. Pine was packing her favorite strawberry jam and a newly baked batch of scones for the judges in the home-produce pavilion, and Resin and Columbine were busy trying to put Puss'll-do and Pinch into cages and to groom them to look like beautiful house pets instead of wild untamed scavengers.

"I wish we could find Gus," Columbine said eagerly. "Gosh, I bet with Gus we'd win the prize for the most unusual pet. Don't you reckon we would, Resin?"

"Sure we would."

"I wish I knew where he was."

Columbine clasped his hands between his knees and stamped his feet up and down in excitement. "I bet with a goanna we'd scare a few people at the Show, wouldn't we, Resin?"

"Yeah."

Resin was too busy trying to strengthen the wire of Puss'll-do's cage to take much notice of his young brother.

"Shall I go look for him? Shall I?"

"If you like."

Columbine started off and paused.

"Where shall I look, Resin? In the shearing shed?"

"What? No, no! It's no use looking for Gus. He's hiding somewhere. In any case, how are we going to catch him?"

"He can run pretty fast."

"Too fast. If he wants to go to the Show, he'll have to go under his own steam. Come on, give us a hand with Puss'll-do."

The huge old tabby was hunched uncomfortably in his box and glared out at them in disgust.

"Hurry up, you two," Mr. Pine called. "Do you want me to take those two mongrels on the truck?"

"Coming," Resin yelled. "Here, you carry Pinch's cage, Columbine, and I'll take Puss. Gosh, he weighs half a ton, I reckon."

And so at last everything was organized and all five members of the Pine family set off—Dad and Resin in the truck, Mum and Columbine in the car, and Turps with the Dobsons and Miss Strarvy. Miss Lemon had stayed in Upper Gumbowie for the weekend; she was one of the judges in the pet section, and she felt she should arrive at the ground looking as neutral and unbiased as possible.

They were just in time. All entries had to be in place by ten o'clock, and then everything was closed to the public for an hour while the judges made their decisions. After the bustle of the morning it was a long and painful wait. And it wasn't improved when the Pines heard a loud voice that they couldn't mistake coming up behind them. It was Aunt Hester with her two children, Angelina and Cuthbert.

"Ah!" she cried, when she was still twenty yards away. "I thought we'd see you here. I said to Stan, 'I know Harry and Muriel always go to the Show!'"

"So does an old battle-ax I know of," Mr. Pine muttered to himself. Then, aloud, he said "Good morning" to Aunt Hester and excused himself during the general hubbub, so that he could slip off and have a look at the new harvesters.

Aunt Hester was Mrs. Pine's sister. She was bigger and more talkative and thought she was much more important. This was because she had married Mr. Stanley Bellony, who was the Rural Manager of the Instant Insurance Company and who owned an expensive house in Summertown. But Mr. Pine had never been impressed by all this, and often pretended to have trouble pronouncing her name, so that it accidentally sounded like "baloney." All the same, the two families seemed to get on well enough together, except for some strong rivalry at certain times of the year. The Annual Gumbowie Show was one of these.

"Well, what have you entered for this year, Muriel?" Aunt Hester asked. "Pickles and preserves again?"

"No, nothing much this year."

"Butter and homemade bread, I suppose?"

"No."

"Sponge cake?"

"You know I can't bake a decent sponge cake, Hester."

"Well, what then? I'll have to put the stomach pump on to you; it's harder to get anything out of you than it is to squeeze water from a brick."

"What have *you* entered for, Hester?"

"Me? Nothing."

"Oh, go on! You couldn't resist it."

"Well, hardly anything."

"What?"

"A bit of tapestry and embroidery."

"Is that all?"

"Oh, and the open section for homemade biscuits."

"I thought you'd have entered for more than that."

"Well, I did put in three or four lots of homegrown flowers—and two vases in the flower-arrangement section."

"That sounds more like it."

"And the children have entered for one or two things: Angelina for the crochet work and the best-dressed doll, and Cuthbert for pastel drawing."

"What are you aiming for this year—ten prizes altogether? That was what it was last year, wasn't it?"

"Eleven. But what about you, you still haven't told us."

"Oh," Mrs. Pine said, "we've hardly done anything this year."

"But you have entered for something?"

"Only jam and scones."

"Why don't you try something different? You always win those."

"I've only won them twice."

"What else have you brought?"

"Nothing. The children are in one or two things, though. Crystal is in the horses-in-action, and the boys have brought a couple of their pets."

"What pets?"

"Only old Puss'll-do, just for fun."

"Not that huge, scrawny old mongrel tom? Why, the judges'll die laughing. He looks like an old bag of barley with fur on."

"Oh, they just did it to provide a bit of a show really."

"Didn't they bring anything else?"

"Only Pinch."

"Who's Pinch?"

Mrs. Pine laughed. "You ought to know; he branded your leg."

Aunt Hester gave a high-pitched screech of unbelief. "Not that hot-clawed little monster? Oh, Muriel, how could you?"

Mrs. Pine laughed. "It's got nothing to do with me. He belongs to the children."

"Well, I think he ought to be banned. Whatever section did they enter him for? The wildest pet?"

"The prettiest."

Aunt Hester gave another screech. "Prettiest! Ugliest, surely."

"Well, I suppose the children think possums are pretty —in a furry, sharp-faced sort of way."

"But Angelina has entered Lady Snowflake. Fancy putting a smelly old possum in *her* class."

Mrs. Pine was about to ask who Lady Snowflake was, but she remembered just in time that this must be the pedigreed white Persian house cat that Aunt Hester was so proud of and had paid so much for.

"Well, I guess the judges will know best," she said. "Now I think we had better see if the Dobsons have arrived with Crystal and her pony." And she escaped before Aunt Hester could start another conversation.

It proved to be a good day for the Pine family. For the third year in succession Mrs. Pine won first prize for her scones. "The hat trick, Mum," Resin said excitedly, for although he would never say so publicly, he was really very proud of his mother's baking. Then Mr. Pine's pigs were awarded a special blue ribbon for quality and breeding, and one of the calves gained a third prize. But the biggest excitement of all came when the doors of the pet pavilion were flung open and the crowd surged in to see the results of the judging. Resin and Columbine, running along at the head of the wave, stopped short, hardly believing their eyes. For there, pinned clearly on the front of Pinch's cage, was a blue card—first prize for the prettiest pet in the show. But that wasn't all. A little farther along the line of cages loomed the big box especially made to house Puss'll-do; and again there was a card, a red one this time, gleaming prominently for everyone to see, and proclaiming that the dear old tame tom, battle-scarred and half as big as a tiger, had won second prize for the "homeliest pet of the year."

"Resin," he yelled. "Resin! Mum! Resin! Come here, quick! Puss'll-do has won a prize." He jumped about like a yo-yo among the gathering crowd, while his mother and brother stared too.

"Isn't that wonderful?" he said, his eyes like marbles. "Isn't Lemon a beaut judge?"

It was not a wise thing to say.

"Huh," they heard someone say. "What does she know about pets?"

Mrs. Pine looked embarrassed.

"Colin!" she said sharply. Then, seeing Aunt Hester's hat nodding forward through the crowd, she hastily gathered up Resin and Columbine and retreated through the far doors of the pavilion.

After a picnic lunch underneath the trees by the Oval, and after Resin and Columbine had spent all their money except a bent penny on seeing the mysteries of Malgo the Magician and the Hairy Man from the Zambezi and on accumulating a vast assortment of sample bags, cotton candy, space gum, caramels, toffee apples, and the porcelain prizes from three cheap-jack tickets, they all stood at the railings to watch Turps and Ginger in the horses-in-action events. They were not the best pair in the competition, but they made a wonderful picture—the chestnut flanks and streaming tail of the horse shining in the afternoon sun, and Turps' hair and light brown riding breeches blending so well that the horse and the girl seemed to be a single creature.

They galloped beautifully across the Oval with a free, swinging rhythm, but they didn't jump well. Ginger was nervous, and twice her fetlocks smacked hard against the railings as she jumped. But in spite of that the two made such a splendid picture that people cheered and clapped as Turps swung Ginger around for the final run and crouched far forward from the saddle, until she seemed to lie along her neck like a golden lizard.

The old men held their pipes with one hand and stopped smoking as she made her run.

"Rides well, that girl. Look at her."

"Harry Pine's daughter."

"Knows horses."

"Very light on the bit."

"She needs a different horse; the one she's got is a better galloper than a jumper."

And then above the men's came a woman's voice: "There's something wild about her, I always think." It was Aunt Hester. "Something bouncy!"

Angelina answered timidly. "She's pretty, Mummy. She is, and so is her horse."

But Aunt Hester soon put a stop to that. "No horse is pretty, Angel. It's impossible. They're too . . . too horsey!"

She was interrupted by a cry from the crowd. Ginger had again failed to clear the railings in her jump, and this time had struck them so hard that she'd stumbled, and the next moment she and Turps had crashed in a tangle of upward-pointing legs. The ambulance men and veterinary officers raced out toward them, but luckily they were not needed. Ginger was back on her feet in an instant, frightened and wild-eyed, and poor Turps picked herself up slowly, dusting her clothes and limping a little as she walked over to the fence. The fall put her out of the competition, and all she could do after Ginger had been caught was to arrange for Mr. Dobson to drop her off at Bottlebrush Barn on the way home, while she herself flopped down in the car beside her mother. She ached as much from disappointment as from bruises.

"I'm sure I was running second, until that happened," she said bitterly.

"Perhaps it's better not to know," her mother said. "The main thing is that you're not badly hurt. How do you feel?"

"All right. A bit tired and sore."

"Better get you home, I think. A hot bath and then bed."

For once Turps didn't object, and so Mrs. Pine drove off in the car, leaving the two boys to come home in the truck with their father. They stayed on for an hour or more watching the Emergency Fire Service display, and begging a few last pennies from Dad. Then they helped load up the calves and the screaming pigs, gathered Pinch and Puss'll-do from their places of glory among the last admiring stragglers, and climbed into the cabin of the truck.

On the way home the sinking sun burned into the windshield like a bronze fire, but Columbine was too tired to notice it. Dirty, disheveled, and triumphant, he shut his eyes to the glare and planned a victory feast for their two prizewinners riding home jerkily on the tray of the truck behind them.

The water drum

Events on Bottlebrush Farm didn't always start with living things like animals or reptiles. Sometimes they were caused by implements, tools, or bits of farm machinery. Nor were they necessarily involved or complicated. One day Columbine proved that he could have the most horrifying adventures with the simplest things imaginable.

He was playing in the yard with an old tennis ball, when it bounced away toward the harness shed and fell into an open forty-gallon drum. The drum was a kind of tiny water tank. The down pipe from the roof of the shed stopped about a yard from the ground. Whenever it rained the water used to fall with a splash near the door of the shed, so Mr. Pine stood the old drum under it to catch the runoff and prevent any mess.

Columbine, running after his ball, stopped short and peered over the rim of the drum. There was about a foot of water in it, and the ball was bobbing gently on the little ripples it had caused. He stretched his arm to try to grab it, but it was way beyond his reach. He was annoyed to think that such a simple thing could stop his game. He could see the ball plainly less than two feet away, but it might just as well have been on top of the television antenna for all the chance he had of reaching it.

He tried pulling himself up so that he could balance on the rim and reach down farther, but he could never quite manage it. Either the toe of his shoe slipped off the side of the drum, or the rim cut into his armpit so painfully that he had to give up. Plainly he had to have something to stand on. He looked about for a box or bin, but there was nothing handy.

Columbine grew more and more annoyed. Now that he didn't have the ball, it became desperately important for him to play with it. He flounced into the harness shed, kicking aside some old collars and bits of leather; he went through the side door into the barn and threw aside some empty bags as if they were likely to be hiding bins or boxes beneath them; and he walked angrily past the implement shed, glowering at the combines and harvesters. At last, by the side of the chicken run, he saw a box—an old coop, skewed and rickety, with half the nails loose and a couple of boards missing. But it was about two feet square, just the right height for him to stand on to reach down into the drum for the ball.

He dragged the coop across to the harness shed and propped it up against the drum. Then, clutching the rim, he hauled himself up and stood uncertainly, steadying his balance with one hand and reaching far inside the drum with the other. Even now, the ball was an inch or two beyond his reach on the far side. He swished the water with the tips of his fingers, trying to set up little waves that would carry the ball around to him. But it just rocked maddeningly up and down in the same spot. In a fit of anger and determination he thumped the iron sides of the drum with the palms of his hands and then stretched far forward, the tips of his fingers straining to the last inch. His feet pressed back harder and harder. He could almost reach the ball. Another inch. He strained harder. Half an inch. Harder still. The tips of his fingers touched it. A fraction more, and he would . . . Crash! The box, spurned to the last inch by his thrusting feet, tipped backward, and suddenly his feet were jiggling in the air. He gave a convulsive forward heave, teetered on the rim for a second, and then pitched headfirst into the drum.

It was a sickening moment. Instinctively Columbine flung his hands sideways against the wall of the drum as his body fell forward. They held, and he stopped his fall, but his head was only an inch or two from the water.

"Help!" he yelled. "Help me! Help me!"

Nobody heard. He hung there, terrified.

"Help! Help!"

Silence. The pressure began to hurt the palms of his hands, and he could feel his face flushing as he hung there, head downward. His ears began to ring. He struggled for a second to try to lever himself upward, but his hand slipped and his head very nearly slid under the water.

The crown of his hair was suddenly cool and wet.

"Help!" No answer. He filled his lungs and gathered all his strength for a louder shout. "H-e-l-p! H-e-l-p!" He waited. Still no answer.

He arched his back and lifted his head to get his hair clear of the water, but the strain on his arms was unbearable. He had that terrifying feeling that his hands were

84

beginning to slip—a slow, uncontrollable movement downward. His palms felt as if they were on fire. And he knew that within a minute or two his head would start to go under. Then, even if he plunged his hands to the bottom of the drum, his arms wouldn't be long enough to hold his head clear; there wouldn't be enough room for him to turn right over, and he would be jammed there, head downward, until he drowned.

"Help!" he yelled, half sobbing, half screaming. "Help! Help!" At the same time he tried to kick his feet in the air to attract attention, his knees thumping the iron rim of the drum with a thud.

"Help! Help!" He kicked again. "Helrrgbb!" This time his cry ended in a bubbling gurgle.

Out in the milking shed Mr. Pine was bending over one of the suction cups from the milking machine. A rubber tube had split and he couldn't mend it well enough to make it airtight. He would have to send one of the children down to Old Barnacle's store for a new piece of tubing. He stood up, undecided. Perhaps it could wait until lunch. No, better do it now, because if Barnacle didn't have one he would have to drive into Upper Gumbowie. The machine had to be working again for the afternoon milking.

He walked out into the cow yard and called. There was no response. He stood listening for a minute. The morning was full of farmyard noises, but not a hint of children anywhere.

"Kids!" he said under his breath. "When you don't want them they're under your feet, but when you need them they're as silent as skinks." He set off impatiently toward the house. As he walked past the back of the harness shed he stopped. Someone was about. Probably

Resin, working on some Heath Robinson invention again, judging by the thuds and thumps. He took another step. No, there were voices too—a queer, garbled kind of war cry. Cowboys and Indians, most likely.

He came around the corner of the harness shed and leaped with fright as he saw a pair of legs disappearing into the water drum. He sprang forward, seized the legs by the ankles, and with one tremendous lift swung Columbine clear of the drum and laid him on the ground beside it.

"Colin!" It was a shout that rang around the farm. Mr. Pine, like his wife, tended to forget about nicknames in moments of crisis. He raised his voice. "Colin, in heaven's name!" He was bending over Columbine, ready to give him mouth-to-mouth resuscitation. But fortunately there was no need. Columbine had only just gone under the water when he'd been hauled out, so his injuries consisted mainly of streaming eyes and nose and paroxysms of coughing that bent him double and sent him blue in the face. His father thumped him on the back, as much from relief and exasperation as from any intention to save his life.

"Colin! What in heaven's name were you doing?"

Colin began to get his breath back. "I . . . I was . . . drying to drab . . . drab the ball."

"The ball?" Mr. Pine was angry and weak and laughing with unbelief. "The ball? So you dived in headfirst?"

"I . . . I fell in. The old box dipped up."

Mr. Pine stood him up and led him, still snuffling and wheezing, to the kitchen. There, after much towel rubbing and scolding from Turps and his mother, Columbine was dried out, dressed in clean clothes, and told to lie down. But he bounced about so much that after ten minutes his mother admitted that he seemed fit enough to get up again, and sent him off with Resin to Old Barnacle's shop.

But Mr. Pine sat down weakly on the sofa and drank three cups of strong black tea. "A couple of minutes!" he kept on saying. "Just a couple more minutes, and I would have been too late."

The end of the year

As the end of the year approached, the tempo of life on the farm quickened. It was one of the annual miracles that Columbine couldn't quite understand, but he knew that it was the most interesting time on the calendar, and he was never disappointed. The school breakup, the harvest, Christmas, the start of a new year, and all the wonderful possibilities of swimming, crayfishing, and exploring during the holidays were enough to set his heart skipping.

This year there was even greater excitement. For Strarvy and Lemon, having announced their engagement on the night of the Gumbowie Ball, which always ended Show Day, now planned to be married on the first Saturday of the school holidays. Nor was that all. Strarvy had been looking about for a house to live in after they were married, and had decided to rent Humpty Doo from Bridget Murphy's father, if Mr. Murphy was willing to have it painted and renovated. This was agreed upon, and so a new interest suddenly appeared almost on Mr. Pine's doorstep. For Humpty Doo was only a mile or two down the road. It was an old four-roomed cottage that had been built years before by an early station pioneer, and then abandoned when the job of clearing The Big Scrub had proved too much for him.

Resin, Donny, Debby, and Turps had often visited Humpty Doo and poked about, looking for relics. Set back a little way in The Big Scrub, it looked down across the rolling valley of Heaslips' farm, and seemed as snug and cool and green-leaved a house as anyone could wish for.

"Jeepers," Turps said over the tea table just before school broke up. "Fancy someone living in Humpty Doo again."

"Will Strarvy keep on driving the school bus?" Resin asked.

"Yes," Mr. Pine said. "The house should be ready toward the end of January. Then when Mr. and Mrs. Harvey come back from their honeymoon, they'll move in. And when school opens in February, they'll start the bus run from Humpty Doo instead of from Dobsons'."

"Yes, but what about us?" Columbine asked in alarm. "We'll be left behind."

"No, numskull," Resin said impatiently. "Dad means that Strarvy will start from Humpty Doo in the mornings, drive *back* as far as Dobsons' to pick us up, and then go on to Gumbowie. It'll only be a few miles farther."

"It'll be funny," Turps said thoughtfully, "to have no Lemon at school next year."

Columbine's eyes opened at the realization. "Won't we have Lemon anymore?"

"Not as Miss Lemmen," his mother said. "She's going to go on teaching, so she tells me, but she'll be Mrs. Harvey then."

"That'll cause some strife," Mr. Pine said, laughing, "to have Miss Strarvy and Mrs. Harvey on the same staff."

"Can we go to the wedding?"

"We've all been invited. It's at four o'clock on the Saturday before Christmas. And the reception is in the Gumbowie Hall."

The excitement increased as the day of the wedding approached. During the last week Strarvy grew more and more absentminded. On the last Monday morning of the term, the school bus stalled three miles out of Gumbowie because he had forgotten to fill the tank with gas, and so all the children had to walk the rest of the way. They arrived at school at a quarter to ten, just as the principal was about to call the police to see if there had been an accident.

On Tuesday morning Strarvy forgot to have a shave, and set off from Dobsons' in the bus with whiskers like spikes all over his chin. He discovered his mistake halfway along the track and was so embarrassed and afraid of seeing Lemon that he sneaked into school by the back way and begged the principal to lend him a razor. On Wednesday he forgot to buy Mrs. Dobson's bread, and on the way home left Burp Heaslip stranded in Gumbowie by sending him to the grocer's for a packet of cigarettes and then driving off unthinkingly.

By the time Thursday came around, everyone was joking and slapping him on the back. But all the children liked him because he had always been very fair and firm, and so they had arranged a big surprise for him and

Lemon during the lunch hour. With the help of the other teachers they had decorated the school assembly hall and arranged a concert. Everyone was invited. Strarvy and Lemon sat in the front row with the principal, and all the items were announced as if they were being given especially for them. At the end of the concert the principal made a speech and then, amid tremendous clapping, the head boy and the head girl of the school helped to carry in two huge parcels and asked Strarvy and Lemon to come out to the front.

"A wedding present from the school, with very best wishes for your future happiness." The words were drowned out by the roar of clapping as all the children who had been saving up and bringing their shillings for weeks craned to see what their money had bought.

Strarvy came out to thank them. He fidgeted a good deal, and kept rubbing his chin as if afraid he had forgotten to shave again. Then he and Lemon untied the yards of string and took off acres of paper, and at last revealed the mystery—two beautiful fireside armchairs. Amid squeals of laughter and delight they sat down in them, facing the audience. Strarvy pretended to lean back and snore, and Lemon shook him to wake him up.

It was a very successful assembly and everyone came crowding around afterward to look at the chairs and read the inscriptions on the little silver plaques set in the wooden backrests. *From the pupils of Upper Gumbowie School. With best wishes.*

Strarvy couldn't very well take the two chairs home on top of the school bus, so he arranged for the principal to store them in his house until Humpty Doo was ready. Then school broke up for the holidays and Strarvy set out on the last trip for the year. But this time he didn't stay at Dobsons'. The school bus had to be stored and overhauled in the garage at Gumbowie over Christmas, so Strarvy loaded it up and brought it back into the town with all his honeymoon luggage. Then he booked in at the hotel for the two days until his wedding.

Saturday was a great day. The town was crowded. By four o'clock they had filled the church and overflowed onto the steps and footpaths outside, to watch Lemon, looking more beautiful than ever, arrive with her father and walk slowly down the aisle. Strarvy was waiting at the altar with the best man. He was supposed to be standing quite still, but he kept scratching his chin nervously every now and then to make sure that it was still clean-shaven.

Resin, Turps, and Columbine, Donny and Debby Dobson, Burp Heaslip, and half a dozen of the other children on Strarvy's bus run were all crowded into pews near the aisle, straining to get a good view. Resin and Donny were hoping secretly that Strarvy would drop the ring or forget to say "I do," but everything went smoothly and happily, and before long they were coming back down the aisle as Mr. and Mrs. Harvey.

There was a great wave of jostling, a surge outside the church, a snowfall of confetti, and a good deal of crouching, twisting, and flicking by cameramen, before Strarvy and his wife escaped in the car.

But the end of the day was the best of all. So far as the children were concerned the reception at Memorial Hall was an endless feast of cake, ice cream, and cool drinks, and things like the toasts, speeches, telegrams, and the cutting of the cake were merely interruptions to the main business of eating and drinking.

Then Lemon, who had disappeared mysteriously during the evening, reappeared looking like herself again, and she and Strarvy slowly started to escape toward the door. It was a long process, because at every step or two they were waylaid by someone wanting to kiss Lemon or to shake Strarvy's hand. But at last they worked their way outside to the car.

There was a final flourish of cans and horseshoes, a huge "Just Married" placard appeared out of nowhere, two pairs of old shoes were hitched onto the back bumper, and Mr. and Mrs. Harvey were on their way.

To Resin and Turps, and one or two of the others from the bus run, it was more than the end of the year. When they went back into the hall again, nothing had been shifted, yet everything had changed. The evening had suddenly become meaningless. From now on they knew that things would never be quite the same again.

Emil and the crayfish

The day before Christmas was an endless one. Resin, Turps, and Columbine had long since finished decorating the Christmas tree; the baking was all done, and the house had been cleaned. Nothing was to be touched or eaten, no pets were allowed inside, games and competitions were forbidden because they made a mess. There was to be no cutting-out with scissors or blades, and on no account were visiting children to be welcomed or entertained.

The reasons for all the bans and restrictions were clear enough. Aunt Hester was coming on Christmas Eve. She and Uncle Stan, Angelina and Cuthbert were going to descend on them from Summertown at about six o'clock, and stay on to light candles, exchange presents, and eat for most of the evening.

It was part of an old tradition in Mrs. Pine's family.

No matter what they thought of each other or what they said behind each other's backs, they always exchanged visits at Christmas. And since Aunt Hester was coming to the Pines' for Christmas Eve this year, it was the Pines' turn to go to Summertown on Christmas Day. Thus for Resin, Turps, and Columbine there was no problem about tonight and tomorrow—these were already mapped out. But it was now only nine o'clock in the morning and Christmas Eve didn't start until six in the evening. In the meantime there were nine or ten hours to fill in somehow.

Luckily Burp Heaslip saved the day. He came sauntering past in bare feet and Tom Sawyer pants, carrying a ragged assortment of cans, twine, and sticks, looking like a cross between a peddler and a hobo.

"What about coming down to the dam?" he called.

"What for?" Resin yelled. "Swimming?"

"Crayfishing."

"Ooh," Columbine shouted. "Yeah, let's."

"Got to call in at Barnacle's first. Mum wants a bit of stuff."

"See you there in five minutes," Resin yelled.

"Right y'are."

Less than five minutes later, Resin and Turps came flying into Old Barnacle's shop, with Columbine close behind them, even before Burp had finished his purchases. They helped him pack the groceries into an empty sugar bag and distributed the crayfishing gear evenly among themselves.

"Is it a good day for them?" Resin asked.

"Not bad. Bit murky, but we'll get them."

They were just leaving the shop when old Emil Eckert, obviously in urgent need of something, came in. He always walked bent forward from the waist as if his legs couldn't keep up with the desperate hurry of his body. Today he was kinked into a gooseneck with haste and frustration.

"Barnacle," he cried in his thick voice as he came bursting through the door, scattering the children in his path, "have you got one of dese?"

Old Barnacle stood crustily behind the counter.

"One of what?"

"Sprocket! Harvester sprocket! Like dis one?"

"Broken, is it?"

"Teet' are all broken, see!" Emil slapped the cog down on the counter with a gesture of agony. "Dis morning it happen. Early. I am reaping quick to get d' paddock all finished before Christmas, and den bang! *Quatsch! Kaput!* Everyt'ing is breaking to pieces."

"Elevator jammed, eh?" Barnacle took the broken sprocket and eyed it like a wine taster holding a precious vintage up to the light. "Pity."

"Never mind about dat," Emil said impatiently. "Have you got anudder one?"

Barnacle paused, scratching his sandpapery chin. "Might at that," he said slowly, "just might at that."

He took the ladder and carried it across to the set of hardware shelves on the other side of the shop. After a good deal of shifting and fidgeting to make sure that the ladder was safe, he started climbing. Up past the nuts and bolts on the lower shelf he went, past the pincers and pliers, past the hinges, hammers, punches, and pipe wrenches, until he could reach up and touch the topmost shelf. There he seized a big, flat cardboard box, drew it down level with his chin, and blew a tremendous blast that ballooned out his cheeks until the veins showed like hundreds of little roots. It swept a layer of dust from the lid of the box in a thick cloud that billowed and surged about his head and almost hid him from view. Then he and the dust slowly descended until he was able to step down from the ladder and drop the box on the counter with a thud.

"Now," he said dramatically, "what have we got in here?" He lifted back the lid, slapping it once or twice and setting up another angry little inferno of dust. Through it Emil could see a confused collection of sprockets and pinions of various makes and shapes, some still bright with red paint under the dust, others black or polished, but all of them unused.

"My word," Emil said hopefully. "We might can find one."

Barnacle took the broken one and examined it again. "Ha!" he said suddenly, diving his hand into the tangle of teeth and pulleys. "A Sunshine, I reckon."

"Yes, of course it is a Sunshine, my machine."

"Then this one should be the thing," Barnacle said, fishing out a sprocket and holding it side by side with the broken one.

Emil gave a guttural grunt of delight. "Dat is it! Dat is it!" He seized the two sprockets and turned them over again and again in the palms of his hands. "Yes, dat is wonderful! wonderful!" He looked at sour old Barnacle appreciatively. "My word, Barnacle, you is a good store-keeper. I said to my vife dis morning, 'First I try old Barnacle. What he hasn't got, nobody has got.' And see, I am right." He pulled his heavy purse from his trouser pocket and unclipped the thick metal clasp. "Well," he said convivially. "How much?" Barnacle stood stolidly behind the counter, his face like a mask.

"Thirty shillings," he said.

"T'irty shillings!" For a second Emil was thunder-struck, but then he burst into a raucous laugh. "Hoch," he said, still chuckling gutturally. "You are always having a joke wit' me."

But Barnacle wasn't having a joke at all; he stood there, dour and unsmiling. "Thirty shillings," he repeated.

Emil was aghast. "You . . . you mean it is *true*? T'irty shillings is the real price?"

"Thirty shillings," Barnacle repeated doggedly.

"Hoch! *Donnerwetter!*" Emil shouted angrily. "You t'ink anythink you can charge." He drew himself up men-acingly. "Well I pretty soon show you." He slapped down the new sprocket on the counter so violently that the children thought the teeth would be snapped off like twigs. "You can *keep* your sprocket. I go and get one in Summertown. And only half d' price."

"Please yourself," Barnacle said nonchalantly. "But it'll cost you twice as much to drive there."

Emil turned as he moved off. "And, if it cost me t'ree times as much, I still get him in Summertown. Rather dat, dan give you d' money, bloodsucking Barnacle Bill." And he stomped out of the shop to his truck with a thunder of six-pound boots on the wooden floor and a crashing of doors as he left. A minute later the truck went flashing up the road with engine and gears roaring.

Barnacle shrugged, gathered up his box unconcernedly, and slowly climbed back up the ladder with it. The chil-dren had the feeling that the old shopkeeper was as shrewd and patient as the Old Man of the Sea. The sprockets, like the drills, axles, bearings, and cotter pins on the other shelf, had probably waited twenty years for a sale, and might easily wait another twenty more. But someday, somewhere, someone would need them. And then Old Barnacle's store, which stocked everything, would come into its own.

"Come on," Burp said suddenly. "Let's get going or we'll never catch any crayfish." And the four of them bumped and bundled their way through the door and set off for the dam.

The dam was a big one that Burp's father had built in his paddock near the drive, a little way in from the main road. When it rained, the water from the road and the hillslopes drained down a channel to the gully that had been blocked off by a high bank. The track to Burp's house ran beside the channel till it reached the dam, and then swung suddenly to one side and curved up to the house. Mrs. Heaslip was always telling Burp's father to put a fence or some rails around the dam in case a car forgot to follow the track one dark night and went straight on into the water. But Mr. Heaslip wasn't concerned.

"Tarnation!" he said. "If anyone coming to see me is such an idiot that he can't even follow the track, then he *needs* a bit of cold water to brighten him up."

The crayfish liked the dam. They lived under the stones and ledges, or in the big muddy holes they'd made in the clay bank. Their claws were blue and mottled like smooth porcelain, with jagged saws and sharp nippers as strong as a pair of pliers. Their bony backs were smooth and blue too, tapering to the overlapping plates that curved beautifully into their tails.

Usually they waited, beady-eyed and still, at the entrance to their burrows. When the water was clear you could see them there, with their feelers as alert as cats' whiskers and their front claws folded inward like boys lying on their stomachs with their shoulders raised on their arms.

Sometimes Burp, who was quick and sharp-eyed, would say "Shhhh!" and point to a patch where the crayfish had left the shelter of their holes and stones and were crawling over the muddy bottom looking for food.

Then very slowly and carefully Burp would lower his wire net behind them and drop down his stick or line near their noses. They stayed stock-still for a minute with their feelers up until the stick came too close. Then suddenly there would be a puff of soft mud and a flick of their tails, as they shot backward like jets—into Burp's net. Laughing and crowing, he flicked them up and tossed them onto the bank where Turps and Debby scrabbled and yelped as they tried to pick them up and drop them into the bucket.

But today it was too murky to see any crayfish on the floor of the dam, so Burp set up hand lines for them. He took a lot of string out of one pocket and a lot of rabbit meat from another, and tied some bait to the end of each bit of string. Then everyone took a line and jiggled it so that the meat fell near one of the crayfish holes. After a while, when they could feel the crayfish tugging at the meat, they started to pull up the line very, very gently with the crayfish still clinging to the meat for all he was worth. Then, if they were lucky, Burp quietly slipped in the net and whipped it up from below before the crayfish could let go and escape.

As more and more crayfish were flipped up onto the bank, Columbine leaped and shouted and yelled, trying to get a grip behind their shoulders before they could throw up their nippers and fasten onto his fingers. Once he let out a shrill yell and danced about with a crayfish hanging from his hand, and when he finally shook it free, there was a bead of blood where the nippers had punched through the skin. Columbine was almost crying, but the others tried to pretend it was a joke. "Hands are not so bad," Burp said, "but once I was walking about in the water barefoot and one of them got me just behind the little toe. Phew! Was he rough!"

Columbine stopped wringing his fingers. "Gosh, what did you do, Burp?"

Burp liked having an audience. "He stuck on there all the way out of the dam, and even after that, while I was hopping about on one leg up the bank."

Columbine forgot about his finger and watched Burp, openmouthed.

"Gosh!"

"It felt as though he was cuttin' off my little toe. Claws like wire cutters he had."

"Big?"

"Big! He could have crushed a bottle between them nearly, I reckon."

"Jeepers!"

"And he kept pressing those pliers of his, and I kept hopping about and hollering."

"You couldn't pull him off?"

"Pull him off? Not unless I pulled my toe off too."

"Gosh, couldn't you get his claws open?"

"You ever tried? Couldn't do it with a crowbar hardly, I reckon. Like a clam, they were."

"How did you get him off in the end, Burp?"

Burp brushed his sleeve across his face as if living the agony again. "Well," he said dramatically, "I hauled back with my leg and let go with a kick—like a soccer player trying to get a goal from the center. And there he went, that crayfish, sailin' way over the top of the bank into the crop in the paddock over there."

"Jeepers!"

"Yeah."

"And your toe? How about your toe, Burp?" Columbine was bent double in an agony of anticipation.

"Well, first I thought it was a gonner, flying up over the bank still clamped in that there crayfish's claws."

"Ker-rikey!"

"But then I looked down and, blow me, there's my toe still stuck on my foot—only it's all sort of blue and patchy-looking, with a fair old lump of meat missin' from the side."

"Gor!"

"And you know what?" Burp looked around confidentially and Columbine kept his hand still, spellbound.

"What?"

"I never ever did find that crayfish again. He flew so far into the wheat crop, I don't know if he ever crawled his way back to the dam again."

Columbine's eyes opened wider than ever. "Burp, d- . . . d'you reckon he might *still* be in there, that same old monster crayfish?"

"Could be."

Columbine packed up his things with finality. "Then I'm not staying, Burp. I'm going home."

The others laughed, but started to pack up too. "Reckon it's about time. Must be getting late," Resin said.

Burp looked critically at the sun. "Way past lunchtime."

Turps sprang up and grabbed her can of crayfish. "Is it? Gosh, we'd better hurry. Aunt Hester'll soon be coming."

Burp gathered up his gear more casually. "See you in a couple of days."

"Yes, on Boxing Day. We have to go up to Summertown tomorrow.

"Roger!"

As Burp sauntered off along the track beyond the dam, the three Pines hurried back the way they had come. Behind them, the ripples they'd been making on the water rocked against the shore and died away; the still air settled back around the dam again; and after a while the old blue crane who lived along the creek flew past heavily on his great slow wings. A few minutes later he came back, landed on the bank, and stood there silently like a gray metal statue. The dam and the paddocks and the whole wide countryside were still and peaceful again.

"We're too late for lunch," Turps said.

"Nev- . . . never mind," panted Columbine, struggling to keep up. "If . . . if we are too late for lunch, we . . . we can eat all the more tonight."

"If Mum'll let us."

They were nearing the main road, and their house was only a few hundred yards away, when a truck came careering down from the north like a dusty willy-willy and rushed up to Barnacle's store. It was Emil Eckert, back from Summertown. Guessing what had happened, the three children ran along the fence and padded barefoot onto Barnacle's veranda, just as Emil went clumping up to the counter.

"Well," he said crestfallen, "dem Summertown shops, dey is not as good as yours, Barnacle. Dey never had dis sprocket for me."

Barnacle just stood watching him.

"Zo I will haff to take your one after all," Emil continued.

"You want to buy it?" Barnacle asked curtly.

103

"Vell, of course," Emil said. "I must have d' sprocket or I cannot reap d' harvest. Already nearly all day I have wasted traipsing over the countryside, and d' harvester has been standing idle in the paddock."

Emil screwed up his face painfully at the thought. "And tomorrow it is Christmas and so dere will be no work again."

Barnacle was climbing back up the ladder for the big box. He brought it down laboriously, plumped it on the counter, and took out the precious sprocket.

"There you are," he said, "and next time don't say you can get it in Summertown."

"No, always I will komm to you next time, Barnacle." Emil took out his purse and started fumbling with money. "T'irty shillings, you said?"

Old Barnacle drew himself up disdainfully. "Thirty shillings?" he said sarcastically. "Don't be silly, Emil! Three pounds to you, take it or leave it."

The children heard Emil's explosion. But they were afraid of what might follow, so they crept off and ran for home. A moment or two later they heard a slamming of doors and Emil went roaring off down the road.

"I don't think he bought the sprocket," Turps said. "He came out too quickly."

"He'll probably drive to Melbourne or Adelaide for one." Columbine was panting again.

Resin laughed. "He'll have to hurry then, if he wants to get it before Christmas Eve."

He suddenly jumped aside as a horn blared behind them and a car rolled past in the dust.

"Jeepers!" Turps and Resin yelled together. "It's Aunt Hester! She's here already!" And they ran for the house as fast as they could.

104

Christmas

For once in her life Mrs. Pine's arrangements for Christmas Eve were in confusion. Her husband was still out working in the paddocks, Aunt Hester had arrived much earlier than expected, and the children had chosen this moment, of all times, to come home late and dirty from the dam.

For as Aunt Hester and Uncle Stan, Angelina and Cuthbert stepped out of the car, Resin, Turps, and Columbine came puffing up the track in their bare feet and crayfishing clothes. Dust from the road and mud from the dam covered their legs and arms, and their hands smelled of rabbit-meat bait and crayfish. Turps' can was a heaving mass of scrabbling blue claws, flipping tails, beady eyes, and long thin feelers.

Angelina minced up in a white nylon dress and peered into the can. "Ooooooh!" she said, catching her throat with her hands as if about to be sick. "Aren't they *horrible*."

"Quite nice to eat," Resin said nonchalantly. "If you like, we'll cook them and have them for supper later."

Angelina put her handkerchief over her mouth. "Don't, Melton! *Please!* I'll be *sick*."

Mrs. Pine came hurrying out to break things up. "Here, you three disgusting tramps," she said sternly, "into the bathroom this instant. I'll give you ten minutes, the lot of you."

She sighed as she turned apologetically to Aunt Hester. "Children! Trust them to choose the wrong time for everything. Oh, Resin," she called just as the three renegades were disappearing into the bathroom.

"Yes, Mum?"

"As soon as you've finished, run and tell your father that the Bellonys are here."

"Righto!"

But Aunt Hester was in a very jovial Christmas-Eve mood. "Never mind, Muriel," she said magnanimously. "Your job is so much harder than mine. If you only lived in town, with a husband who wore white shirts, you could have things so much *easier*. Look at Angelina and Cuthbert. I haven't changed their clothes all day."

"I don't know that I'd want to swap," Mrs. Pine said tartly. Then, feeling that they were starting badly for the season of peace and goodwill, she bustled them all inside to plates of cakes, bowls of nuts, and limitless bottles of cold ginger beer. By the time it grew dark, and the Christmas candles had been lit, the two families were singing carols together like the friends and relations they really were. But it was too much to expect that everything would go smoothly. In the first place, Resin almost started

106

a stampede by guilefully suggesting to Cuthbert that perhaps he'd like to see how tame Pinch really was. Cuthbert at once blurted out the news.

"Oooh, Dad, did you hear? Melton's going to show us his pet possum. It's as tame as anything now and it can . . ."

Nobody ever heard what it could, because at that moment Cuthbert was cut short by a dish-rattling shriek from his mother

"The *possum*! Keep him away! Keep him away!" She was standing in the corner, clutching her dress tightly around her legs, peering from side to side. "Muriel, keep that beast away! Keep him away!"

Resin's mother was angry. "Melton, don't you dare bring that animal in here; where is he?"

"Outside."

"Where outside?"

"In his cage."

"Well, what's Cuthbert talking about?"

"I just asked him if he wanted to see Pinch, that's all."

"Don't be so stupid! You know what happened to Aunt Hester last time."

There was no need to remind anyone. Aunt Hester kept up such a vivid description of her ordeal for the next ten minutes that Uncle Stan and Mr. Pine began to hope that Pinch would accidentally escape and start another scene of riotous panic. But at last she simmered down. The presents, which had been heaped tantalizingly around the foot of the tree, were distributed, and there was a great deal of paper-rustling, shouting, thanking, admiring, exclaiming, and even kissing while the presents were unwrapped, held up, and handed around for everyone to see.

107

"Just what I've always wanted," everyone said to everyone else, whether it was true or not—everyone, that is, except Mr. Pine, who was too honest to be insincere and who stood, with a look of desperate resignation, holding yet another fiercely colored tie from Aunt Hester.

"Now," Mrs. Pine cried above the sound of jubilation, "we'll each share a Christmas cracker and then I'll get supper." She turned quickly to Turps. "Crystal"—it was always Crystal in front of visitors—"run and get the crackers from the sideboard."

"I'll get them," Columbine yelled shrilly; "please, can I get them?" He was off like a rabbit.

"And find something to put them in," his mother called after him. "A box or can or something, so that each person can help himself."

"All right."

Columbine was so anxious for the excitement and mystery of the crackers that he rushed into the dining room, seized an armful of them, and dashed out again before his mother's message really reached him. As he moved past the semidarkness of the laundry door, however, he realized the need for a container; so he turned, dropped his whole load into a bucket, and carried it hastily up to the living room.

Then, holding the bucket up at elbow height, he offered the crackers around, each person thrusting a hand in like a customer at a lucky dip. Aunt Hester was busy with talk as usual when it came to her turn, but the whole house knew instantly that she was involved in some kind of disaster again.

"Eeeeeeeek!" The well-known shriek shrilled through the house, jarring Turps' teeth like fingernails scratched across galvanized iron. "Eeeeeeek! Eeeeeeek!" The next minute Angelina's voice joined her mother's. "Eeeeeeeek! Eeeeeeeek!" Everyone jerked around to see, and this time even Mr. Pine was genuinely startled.

For hanging from the point where Aunt Hester's finger and the Christmas cracker met, was the biggest blue-nipper crayfish in Turps' collection. He had fastened securely onto both the cracker and a bit of Aunt Hester's skin with one claw, and was thrashing about angrily with his legs and feelers, while poor Aunty thrust her arm out from her body like a wooden scarecrow, leaning far over and redoubling her shrill shrieks.

"Hang on, Aunty!" Resin yelled, rushing up. "I'll get him."

But as Aunt Hester pointed out shrilly afterward, it wasn't *she* who had to do the hanging on; the crayfish was doing that quite effectively. Even Resin had a hard time trying to separate them, and it wasn't until he'd pried open the crayfish's claws with a meat skewer that he managed to free the pinched finger. Really it was no more than a needle prick, with a little bead of red blood where the sharp nipper had punctured the skin, but no doubt it hurt a good deal and seemed much worse than it really was. At any rate, Aunt Hester made it sound that way. She wrung her hand and went off, wailing, to the medicine chest with Mrs. Pine to find antiseptic, cotton wool, and adhesive plaster. When she returned, she was as noisy as a bucketful of stones.

"If it's not possums, it's crayfish," she yelped. "Every time I visit the Pines something attacks me."

Uncle Stan pretended to be concerned so that he wouldn't seem to be enjoying himself too much. "It is getting dangerous, Hester," he said. "There are always animals and reptiles waiting to take you by surprise."

109

But Mrs. Pine was terse. She was afraid Aunt Hester would think that these accidents were deliberate; she wasn't even sure herself whether the children were playing some kind of clever practical joke.

"Colin," she said severely. "Come here."

Columbine shuffled up and stood before her, hanging his head.

"Now, young man, would you mind telling me how the crayfish happened to get mixed up with the Christmas crackers?"

"It was in there."

"What do you mean, it was in there?"

Resin felt he must come to the rescue of his young brother. "They are all in there. Look!" He held up the bucket revealing the creaking scrabble of crayfish in the bottom. "It was the crayfish can, the one we used at the dam today."

Mrs. Pine looked even more severe. "Then how did it come to have the crackers in it?"

"I don't know." Columbine was wide-eyed with innocence. "I didn't know it was the bucket."

"For heaven's sake, talk sense, Colin! What didn't you know?"

Resin tried to interpose again, but his mother silenced him sternly.

"Well?"

"You said put them in a can or something, you said so." Poor Columbine felt somehow he was getting onto very slippery ground.

"Put *what* in a can?"

"The crackers. You said. And I was carrying them all, when you said it, and I went into the laundry and . . . and . . . and I put them straight into the bucket and I

110

brought the bucket out, and it had all the crayfish in the bottom of it, underneath, and I didn't know it at all. No, I didn't know!"

Columbine stopped, breathless and self-righteous, waiting anxiously to see if his obvious innocence had finally appeased his mother and calmed the long thin anger of Aunt Hester. Luckily it amused Dad.

"Well, that beats all," he suddenly roared, shaking with laughter. "If you'd left him alone, Muriel, he would have brought all the crackers in without any fuss. But because you wanted them in a can, you got crayfish and all, like a lucky dip."

Uncle Stan burst into laughter too. "Lucky nip, more likely, wasn't it, Hester?"

And although Aunt Hester still didn't think it was anything to joke about, she could see there was no point in making a fuss over it, especially on Christmas Eve. So everyone joined in singing more carols, eating supper, and wishing more good wishes until it was time for the Bellonys to go home. Even that was only an interlude.

"See you for Christmas dinner tomorrow," Aunt Hester cried shrilly as they drove off, "and don't be late."

"No. We've got four and twenty possums baked in a pie," Uncle Stan added, "and lots of live crayfish in the plum pudding. Better watch out for nips on the noses." He drove off laughing, with everyone waving and calling out.

Mr. and Mrs. Pine and the children stood outside watching the lights of the car recede up the Summertown road. It was a still, warm night. Overhead the great arch of the sky was picked with stars as clear as chips of ice; it seemed as if Australia and the whole world beyond it to the hills of Bethlehem itself must be lying calmly under that bending arch tonight. Perhaps at last for a moment there was peace on earth and goodwill among men.

The next day the Pines repaid the visit. Summertown baked in the midday heat, but Aunt Hester even had the weather under her heel. She had a big electric air conditioner working full blast in the dining room, and the blinds were all partly drawn. The refrigerator and freezer, stocked to bursting point during the past week, now disgorged their vast vats full of jellies and salads, ices and trifles, bottles and cream, junkets and ham, until the dining table seemed to tremble and sag with the load. And in the middle of the whole affray Aunt Hester stood like a railway signal post—tall, thin, and dominating—sending out messages with her jabbing bony arms. That was why Uncle Stan was stationed at his post, carving prodigious cuts from two whole turkeys, and why Angelina danced a minuet around the table with loaded plates, and Cuthbert stood an army of bottles to attention on the servery shelf with a vanguard of glasses marching rigidly in front of them.

It was a tremendous Christmas dinner, one of those huge turkey-and-gravy-and-seasoning-and-six-different-vegetable kinds of dinners that always put Columbine out of action long before the interesting things arrived. But when it was all over, Resin, Turps, and Columbine suddenly felt that things had come to a dead end. There was nowhere to go—no sheds to play in, no dam to swim in, no Big Scrub to explore. Outside, the asphalt street, shimmering and melting into tackiness, ran straight and wide through the center of the town, past the shops and the houses with the white picket fences and the small trapped beds of flowers and handkerchief lawns. But nobody moved today, not even a dog. The street was bare, empty,

112

lifeless. And so, after a brief, barren excursion down the pavement the children retreated to the ear-thickening rumble of Aunt Hester's air conditioner, and the soft comfort of her inch-deep carpet.

There they stayed until the late afternoon when, after another bout of eating that Mr. Pine said was quite rich and unnecessary enough to make them all bilious, they set off home to their waiting farmyard and empty water troughs.

"It's just as well," Mr. Pine said, slackening the belt on his old working trousers, "that Christmas comes only once a year. Otherwise the people would all be dead from overeating, and the animals from starvation and neglect."

Holidays

For the next four weeks, Resin, Turps, and Columbine lived the kind of life they thought children ought to be allowed to live all the time. They ranged about with their father in the far paddocks while the harvest came in; they carried lunch and water bags, rode on trucks, cleaned out chutes, stored sacks, went barefoot, and helped to pick and preserve the orchard fruit. They wore shirts and shorts and old straw hats, and the skin of their arms was the color of toast. They went for trips with Don and Debby Dobson, and they paddled in Burp Heaslip's dam, where the mud squeezed up between their bare toes like plasticine.

Twice they saw fires. Once it was a scrub fire far off to the east—a thick stain against the sky like dirty steam that set all the phones ringing and the Emergency Units racing off. But luckily it was held within a mile or two and there wasn't much damage. The second one was a grass fire in open country near Gumbowie. They were just starting back from a Saturday shopping trip when the alarm sounded and the men of the Gumbowie Unit came running like Air Force pilots racing to their planes. The fire was sweeping over a hill a mile beyond the town, and Mr. Pine stopped his car on the side of the road so that he wouldn't hinder the fire trucks as they went roaring past.

The children had a bird's-eye view of the battle, with their father beside them to point out what was happening. It was the first time they had ever seen a Fire Unit in action against a real fire, and they scarcely knew whether to be thrilled or terrified.

"Saint George and the Dragon!" Turps exclaimed. "Look!"

A long red line of fire was sweeping over the crest of the hill and a fire truck was racing up to intercept it at the point where the edge of the blaze began.

"Yes," Mr. Pine said grimly. "Luckily the dragon's wings are clipped today. He's out in the open in short grass, and there isn't any wind."

"Look at the truck! It's making short work of the fire. Just look at it go."

It was true. The water tender roared up toward the advancing red line and swung along beside it. Suddenly a great jet of water shot out at the fire and the flames faltered and sank. The truck moved along quickly, leaving behind a black smoking strip where the fire had been.

"Hah!" Resin cried excitedly. "Look at them mowing down the flames. It's just like a machine gun with a stream of water for bullets."

Two men held the powerful nozzle and kept aiming it

115

at the fire as they went along. Other men leaped off and put out the embers and flaring remnants with beaters, sacks, and knapsack sprays. They were smothering the fire at the rate of five miles an hour. From the other flank came a second fire truck, roaring in low gear with a full water tank, belching out an even stronger stream of water. The tall red petals of flame disappeared in an instant, and shriveled up into blackened cinders. The two trucks lumbered toward one another, eating up the line of fire between them. Before the blaze had traveled halfway down the hill, the trucks met, and the fire was quenched. All that remained was the mopping up, as Mr. Pine put it, and careful patrolling for the rest of the day to see that it didn't flare up again.

Turps was wide-eyed with enthusiasm. "That was wonderful, Dad," she cried, "just wonderful. I didn't know the E.F.S. could be so fast and strong."

Columbine, too, was agog. "They pretty soon fixed that old fire, didn't they, Dad? I bet they could fix any bushfire in the world."

But their father was cautious. "They were lucky. There wasn't much for the fire to feed on, and there wasn't any wind. But in another ten minutes it would have been down in Eckert's wheat crop, and soon after that in the Forestry Commission's pine plantation. Then the red dragon would have started to show his claws."

But Turps didn't want to leave the scene on such an ominous note. "I thought it was wonderful all the same," she cried, "the way the men fought."

"So it was, so it was," her father said as he started the car and moved off for home. "The E.F.S. fellows are always battlers. But fire is like disease; prevention is better than cure."

116

Behind them the fire-swept knoll of the hill, bare and black and menacing, warned the children that Dad was right.

Toward the end of January there was much excitement near Bottlebrush Barn. Strarvy and Lemon came back from their honeymoon and started to move into Humpty Doo. Resin, Turps, and Columbine watched everything with interest and amazement, sometimes from the shelter of The Big Scrub when they thought they were becoming unwelcome nuisances, sometimes from close at hand when they knew their help was appreciated. And so, while Lemon stood in agonized indecision over the position of a table or couch or cupboard, and poor Strarvy sweated and struggled to rearrange the furniture to meet his wife's entreaties, the children fetched and carried, chopped and swept, cleaned and fastened, according to her varying directions. And at least twice a day one or other of them had to trek down to Old Barnacle's store for supplies, according to the emergency of the moment. Nails and sandpaper, cheese and paint, putty and biscuits, tea, screws, washers, butter, flywire, and pegs—all of these and a dozen more were suddenly needed urgently, and always one at a time.

Yet the children loved the jobs they did, and watched each new development with almost as much pleasure as the newlyweds themselves. Especially Turps. She ooh-ed over the curtains and ah-ed over the cushions, like Lemon herself. And when Strarvy came driving out from Gumbowie one day in an old jalopy he'd bought, tooting the horn and roaring the engine, the children rushed out with Lemon, cheering and shouting with joy. For perched on top of the hood, tied down precariously with rope and string and sacking, were the two fireside armchairs that the schoolchildren had given them as a wedding present. Resin helped Strarvy lift them down and carry them inside, and then waited until Lemon fiddled with their positions and tested their comfort.

But the biggest delight of all was Lemon's pet canary. It lived in a big wire cage on the veranda and either whistled furiously when the mood took it or sat silently and cheekily with its head on one side and a knowing look in its eye.

"What's he called, Miss Lemon?" Columbine asked.

"Mrs. Harvey, Colin."

Columbine wrinkled his nose in baffled astonishment. "Mrs. 'Arvey?"

"Yes. Not Miss Lemon."

"What?"

Strarvy roared with laughter as Colin turned to him, quite bewildered. "That's a funny name for a canary."

Strarvy doubled up. "She means *her* name, Colin. It's not Miss Lemon anymore. It's Mrs. Harvey."

The light of discovery lit up Colin's eyes, but the main mystery was still unsolved.

"Well, then, what's the canary called?"

"Mr. Whistle," Strarvy told him.

"No, it's Mr. *Whistler*," Lemon said decisively.

"It's a good name," Turps said. "It suits him."

"Good! Now all we need is a cat."

Columbine stampeded her with offers. "Flopsy's got kittens, four of them. You can have one, Miss Lemon."

"Mrs. Harvey."

"Oh, yes, Miss Harvey."

"Mrs."

"Yes, Mrs."

118

"And one looks just like Puss'll-do. I reckon he's the father, Miss Lemon."

"Mrs. Harvey."

"Yes, Mrs. Harvey. And one's a gray-and-white, and one's sort of nothing much, and one's got just a teeny tip of white on his ear, and one's got fleas. Do you want one?"

"He means do you want a *kitten*, dear," Strarvy said dryly.

Lemon seemed to have trouble with her throat for a second, but in the end she thanked Columbine very much for his offer and said she'd love to have whatever kitten he'd like to pick out for her.

That was how it came about that Strarvy and Lemon had both a cat and a canary. And now the blue wood smoke rose up each morning from the chimney of Humpty Doo, and the doors and gables shone with new paint, and six hens scratched about under the shady trees all around. For Humpty Doo was a home again, not just an old house, and Strarvy and Lemon seemed as happy and excited there as two pigeons in a nest.

Before long the holidays were over and it was time to go back to school. Although the children liked school-work well enough, it was always a trial to put on shoes and socks again just when the heat of February was starting to bake the land.

There was a flurry of scrubbing and rubbing on the night before, to say nothing of the frantic search for schoolbooks and cases, pencils and erasers, rulers and lunch boxes, so that by the time the first day of the term arrived, the Pines and the Dobsons, the Eckerts and Wilsons, Burp Heaslip and Bridget O'Brien were all waiting

119

at their bus stops as clean and bright as starched hats.

It was strange at first to see Strarvy come hurrying past from the wrong direction, but they soon grew used to it. In fact it served as an alarm clock to warn them when they were running late.

"There goes Strarvy," someone would yell as soon as the bus came snorting up the road from Humpty Doo and rattled past the gate of Bottlebrush Barn on its way up to the Dobsons. "He'll be back with Donny and Debby in five minutes."

It was always the signal for a last-minute spurt. Mrs. Pine hustled with Turps' hair ribbons, Columbine banged down the lid of his case, and Resin hurled a bundle of cabbage leaves into the rabbit hutch. Then, often with a shoelace undone or a piece of toast half-eaten, they'd run for the gate just as Strarvy came rumbling up.

"Indigestion again," he called cheerily. "Why don't you get up earlier?"

"We do," Turps would answer, panting, "but the time goes quicker every morning."

Lemon seldom came with Strarvy on the little reverse trip to Dobsons'. Instead, she used Strarvy as an alarm clock too, and stayed behind at Humpty Doo hastily making the bed and clearing the breakfast dishes before he came back down the road on the run into Gumbowie. Then she tritted and trotted hurriedly out to the bus in her high heels.

"Ah, we've got a new girl! What class are you in at school, dearie?" Strarvy called as his wife climbed on board and playfully cuffed his ear, while the children rollicked on their seats with mirth.

And so the new school year started. It was the middle of February. The asphalt in the school yard blistered in the heat, the windows glared, the woodwork cracked. Outside on the farms and stations the livestock panted under the drooping trees, the stubble was drier than wood-wool, the scrub as brittle as matchsticks.

All over Australia the February Dragon was straining at his leash.

Aunt Hester's picnic

At last Aunt Hester's visitors arrived. They drove up to Summertown from Melbourne one Friday afternoon and arranged to stay until the following Monday morning. There were five of them—Aunt Hester's cousin Harold, his wife Audrey, and their three children. They were really six weeks overdue with their visit, because they'd originally planned to come on New Year's Day, but the trip had been postponed four times by sickness and emergencies.

Aunt Hester rushed out to welcome them, semaphoring wildly with her long bony arms.

"Hullo, Harold! Hullo, Audrey! You're here!"

"At last," Harold groaned, climbing out stiffly.

"How are you? How are you?" Aunt Hester was a great one for repeating everything twice.

"Fine! Fine!" Audrey said, unconsciously doing the same.

Uncle Stan stood like a small post behind his tapering signal tower of a wife.

"Have a good trip?"

"Hot and dusty."

"Better come in and cool off."

Aunt Hester rushed in to prevent Uncle Stan suggesting something on his own account. "Come in! Come in! Bring your suitcases and things. It's too hot to stay out here in the street." She led the way urgently up to the veranda like a hurrying stick insect.

"You and Audrey take the spare room, Harold. Young Helen can share Angelina's room, and the two boys can have the porch."

And so, with everything organized, Aust Hester swept into action. The only thing that disappointed her was that the visitors were staying for such a short time.

"Couldn't you stay just a little bit longer?" she pleaded for the tenth time. "Say, for a week?"

"No, not now that the new term has started. The children have to get back to school."

"Well, we'll have to pack so much more into one weekend," Aunt Hester said resignedly. "Tonight a lot of our friends are coming around." Uncle Stan and Cousin Harold sighed, but Aunt Hester pressed on, jerking her hands and setting the pendants on her earrings tumbling like acrobats. "Tomorrow morning we're going out to Booborowie Station—our friends the Marshalls run it, you know—and in the afternoon there's tennis, and at night the Bridge Club's Annual Fête."

This time even Audrey sighed, but Aunt Hester didn't notice.

"On Sunday morning we'll all go to church, and then on Sunday afternoon and evening we'll finish up with a chop picnic out at the Red Gums."

"Where are the Red Gums?" Cousin Harold asked listlessly.

"In Rowett's Reserve. It's a picnic spot, near The Big Scrub."

"The big what?"

"Scrub! It's just a local name."

Uncle Stan rasped his throat. "Uncleared land," he said. "Some is State Reserve, some is private property. Thirty or forty miles of it, all the way down to Gumbowie."

Aunt Hester was as enthusiastic as a laying hen. "Rowett's Reserve is a lovely place, Harold. You'll love it." Her earrings bounced. "Especially for a chop picnic."

"Can we have a chop picnic at this time of the year?" Harold asked. "Are we allowed to light fires?"

Aunt Hester signaled delightedly. "Oh, yes, they've got special fireplaces there, all set out. It's lovely."

"What if there's a total fire ban?"

"Oh well, that's different." Although Aunt Hester was slightly crestfallen, she brightened quickly. "But that's not often; we'll be all right on Sunday. And it's such a lovely place. You'll see."

And they did see. On Sunday afternoon the two carloads of picnickers pulled up in Rowett's Reserve under the big gum trees and started unloading.

"Whew!" Uncle Stan and Cousin Harold said together. "It's a scorcher."

But Aunt Hester would not allow anything to spoil the fun she thought everyone should be having. "It's a nice clear heat," she said decisively, "and there's no wind."

"All the same it *is* hot," her husband insisted. "Especially out by the fireplaces. What'll it be like when we get the fire going?"

Audrey agreed. "There's not a bit of shade by the fire-places. Why didn't they build the things under the trees?"

"Safer out in the open, I suppose," Cousin Harold said. "No danger of fires."

"Safer," Uncle Stan agreed, "and better in winter and spring. The fireplaces and the chop eaters don't have to have a cold shower every time the wind blows."

Harold laughed. "I know; dripping leaves splashing drops as big as dinner plates down your neck." He paused. "All the same, I wish they'd put one of the fireplaces near a tree—for shade in the summertime."

Uncle Stan was curt. "You're not supposed to have chop picnics in the summer." He screwed up his face. "Who wants to eat a greasy chop on a day like this, anyway. The fat's dripping off it before you start."

"That's an idea! Spread them out in the sun. Solar chops."

Aunt Hester came bustling out with a carton of plates, knives, chops, sausages, butter, loaves of bread, and tomato sauce. Luckily she hadn't heard them. "We'll grill them here in the shade," she said. "It'll be much nicer."

"But there's no fireplace."

"Oh, for goodness' sake, Stan!" She was getting impatient. "We'll make a campfire here and do them on the griddle iron." She turned to the children. "Cuthbert! Angelina! Run and gather up some leaves and sticks and things. We want to grill the chops."

Cousin Harold held his paunch in his hands and stood hesitatingly, his head on one side. "Are you allowed to light a campfire here?"

"Well, why not? That's what Reserves are for."

"But you're supposed to use the proper fireplaces."

Aunt Hester was losing patience. "For heaven's sake,

125

Harold, haven't you and Stan been saying that it's too hot out there? I'm only trying to please everyone, that's all."

She flounced off to direct the children, who were coming back with bundles of sticks, leaves, and small logs.

"Over here, Cuthbert! Just here, see?" She waited until the pile was in place. "Now, get some stones, big ones if you can, and we'll build a border to rest the griddle on."

"I still don't know whether it's the right thing, Hester," Uncle Stan began.

"Oh, stop fussing, Stan! Anybody would think you didn't *want* to have a picnic."

Uncle Stan was picturing his cool house at home, with the foam-rubber couch, and the refrigerator full of cold things, but he didn't say anything. When his mind returned from its daydreaming, his wife was still talking. "Nobody is more careful than I am," she was saying aggressively, "when it comes to fire. If everyone else was half as thorough, there'd never be any bushfires. Stan, give me your matches."

The spurt of flame from the match, yellow-red in the bright daylight, bent and flowed around a dry leaf for a second. Then, in an instant, it raced up through the pile of leaves and shot out through the top in a twisting spiral of smoke and fire like the genie leaping from Aladdin's lamp. "Look at *that*," Cousin Harold said. "No trouble getting things to burn today."

"It's like gunpowder." Uncle Stan picked up a stick and poked a few straying twigs back into the circle of stones that the children had made. "Shouldn't be hard to grill the chops."

Aunt Hester was already getting the bread. As soon as the first fierce flare had died down, she piled some heavier

126

logs on the fire and waited until they were gleaming with red coals. Then she set the grilling iron over them and the chop part of the picnic began. But in spite of all her energy, Aunt Hester had to admit that things didn't go with a swing. The flies soon settled over everything in droves, and nobody really wanted greasy chops or sausages, although everyone tried to be very polite about it. But after juggling the hot charcoal-coated meat on a slice of bread for a while, most of the picnickers stealthily dropped it into the fire, pretending that they had gnawed away joyously until there was nothing but bone and gristle left.

Even when the sun set at last, and they tried grilling another batch for tea, there wasn't much enthusiasm. The butter had melted into greasy gobbets floating in yellow syrup, the cool drink was warm, and the lettuce leaves were as limp as rags.

"Well, at least we can have some black billy tea," Aunt Hester said, throwing a handful of tea leaves into the boiling billy on the campfire. She wrinkled her nose and sniffed in like a vacuum cleaner. "Ah, there's nothing like tea out of an old black quart pot; you can smell the gum leaves in it."

They sat drinking tea and talking under the wide sky until eight o'clock, with the big trees thrusting up their leafy crowns around them like dark umbrellas. A slight breeze had sprung up from the north and the leaves stirred gently. The children were playing in the moonlight.

"It's nice out now," Aunt Hester said, in her high, flat voice.

"Best it's been all day," Cousin Harold admitted. "What was the temperature?"

127

"Ninety-seven," Uncle Stan called. He had been listening to the news on a transistor radio. "And it'll be hotter tomorrow—over a hundred, they forecast."

Cousin Harold clicked his teeth. "Then we'd better get an early start. Before five o'clock. I don't want to drive all the way back to Melbourne with my pants stuck to the seat."

Uncle Stan laughed. "We'd better clear up and set off home. You'll need a good rest before a long trip like that."

Packing up was Aunt Hester's business again. And so was the dousing of the campfire.

"Scatter it first," she said, supervising the boys as they poked and kicked the coals apart. "Then heap sand and dirt around it if you can, and last of all get some water from the tap by the toilets."

"What about the log?" Cuthbert asked, prodding and panting as he tried to shift part of a limb they'd pushed into the campfire. It was still four or five feet long and ought to serve several more picnics before it was done.

"I'll douse it with water from the billy," Aunt Hester said. "Stand back."

There was a furious commotion of hissing steam in the night as the red coals were suddenly blacked out like a light being switched off. A turmoil of white smoke boiled up and slowly dispersed among the trees in the moonlight, until only a few vague wisps faltered and curled above the blackened coals.

"That's done it," Aunt Hester said. "And it only took five minutes. It's a pity everyone isn't as thorough as that. But some people never learn."

She picked up the last few odds and ends from the picnic and climbed into the car. "Come on, Stan! We're ready.

The two cars drove out of the picnic ground and the red wink of their taillights faded into the distance. In Rowett's Reserve everything was still. Hours went by. A possum skittered across the ground, sniffing for scraps; a nightjar swished overhead on hushing wings; a plover called far away beyond The Big Scrub. And the breeze rose. After a week of still heat, the weather was building up to another summer peak with a northerly like the breath of a furnace.

The wind swung the crowns of the big trees in the Reserve and dusted them against the night sky like mops. It swept up dust and scraps of paper and fallen leaves. It blew strongly and urgently over the site of Aunt Hester's dead campfire and smoothed itself around the blackened end of the limb she'd doused.

And it found fire!

Far underneath the curve of the limb, hidden away like a red vein among the black charred coals at the end, fire still lived. The water from Aunt Hester's billy had splashed over the top of the log and run down the sides amid the steam and smoke. In many places it had trickled right around and put out the underside as well. But not in one place. And she hadn't turned the log over. Yet even if she had, she might not have seen the fire sleeping there under the black and shrinking coals, hidden and buried in the warm flesh of the wood.

And now, just before morning, with the bellows of the north wind blowing on it and fanning it patiently hour by hour, the red streak began to squeeze out between the charred coals again, and to spread slowly along the under-

129

side of the limb. By daybreak the round limb was barred with red like a snake's belly, sinuous and angry along the ground.

The trees in The Big Scrub tossed in the rising wind. The birds called hastily; the animals fidgeted, ill at ease. Perhaps they sensed something stirring down at Rowett's Reserve.

For Aunt Hester had left the cage door ajar, and now the February Dragon was sniffing at the chink.

The Dragon set free

On Monday morning, Resin, Turps, and Columbine were running late again.

"Five more minutes," their mother called. "Strarvy's bus is on the way up to Dobsons'."

Then the panic began.

"Where's my school case?"

"My blue hair ribbon's missing."

"Have you fed the rabbits?"

"What have we got for lunch?"

"Mum, I need sixpence for a new exercise book."

"Can we buy a bottle of Coke? It's going to be awfully hot today."

There was a scatter of arms, legs, and tongues, Resin flung a bundle of chard to the rabbits, and Columbine spilled milk all over the floor in his hurry to feed Puss'll-do, Flopsy, and the kittens.

"For goodness' sake, watch what you're doing," Turps cried, accidentally treading in the mess and leaving white footprints across the kitchen.

"Crystal, is Ginger still locked in her stable?" Mrs. Pine called from the veranda.

"Yes."

"Better let her out before you go."

"Oh, gosh," Turps said, running about feverishly. "Could you do it for me, please, Mum?"

"She's your horse, dear; you must learn to look after her."

"Yes, but the bus'll be here in a second."

"You know the bargain we made."

"*Please*, Mum."

"I'm busy myself, dear. I have to drive over to Ochre Flat for lunch today—it's the annual C.W.A. meeting."

"Here comes Strarvy," Resin called. "Come on or we'll miss the bus."

"Oh Jiminy!" Turps grabbed her case and ran for the door. "Tell Dad to let Ginger out, will you, Mum?"

"Your father has been over at Heaslips' since daybreak, stacking bales.

"Will *you* then? *Please*, Mum! I haven't got time, really I haven't. Strarvy gets hopping mad when we're late. 'Bye."

Columbine ran past her and Resin loped after him. "G'bye Mum! 'Bye!"

"Good-bye. Don't play out in the heat too much."

Mrs. Pine watched the three figures racing down toward the road as the bus pulled up. She waited until they had climbed on board, then sighed and hurried inside. There was a lot of cleaning up to be done, and she had to get ready for the meeting. First she went through the house, shutting all the windows and drawing all the blinds. The north wind was already blowing hard; by midday it would be like a blowtorch. She made the beds and picked up the scattered trail of debris left by the children's haste and weekend energy. Columbine's train set was still laid out on the passage floor, lying in wait for someone to step on it. Turps' half-finished jigsaw puzzle was arranged hopefully on the dressing table, with the remaining pieces strewn all over it thicker than autumn leaves. And Resin's shorts and old slouch hat still lay by the door where he'd flung them. There were a dozen other jobs waiting too, but Mrs. Pine didn't have time for them all. In any case, the whole place would be covered in dust by the time she got back that night, so there was no point in washing, cleaning, or dusting. She cleared the breakfast dishes, put in a batch of scones to take to the C.W.A. meeting, and lit the bath heater. Although the temperature outside was nearing a hundred, she still didn't like cold baths. As she went to the linen closet for a clean towel she nearly trod on Puss'll-do. He was sprawled out on the cool linoleum, idly licking his paw.

"You fat old nuisance," she said sharply. "Get out of the way!"

Puss'll-do walked casually down the passage for a couple of feet, then flopped down on the floor again. He didn't seem greatly concerned whether she went to her meeting or not.

All over the district the midmorning ached with heat. Old Barnacle Bill slammed his door shut against the dust of the north wind and pulled down the green blind. People knew the shop wasn't really closed; it was just that Barnacle believed semidarkness looked cooler than daylight. At Humpty Doo, Lemon's canary sat listlessly in

133

its cage under the veranda, with its wings drooping and its beak agape. It hadn't even been able to raise any interest earlier in the morning when Lemon had clicked her tongue at it before locking the kitchen door and hurrying off to catch Strarvy and the school bus.

At the Heaslips' farm Burp's father and Mr. Pine stopped loading bales for a minute, wiped their heavy wrists across their foreheads, and flicked off the perspiration.

"What a day to pick," Burp's father said. "Mad dogs and Englishmen go out in the midday sun—them, and a couple of other idiots I know."

Thirty miles south, in her big house at Summertown, Aunt Hester sat near the air conditioner and drank a glass of cold lemonade. Her visitors had left before sunrise, Uncle Stan was at work, and Angelina and Cuthbert were at school. She had stripped the beds, washed the sheets, and tidied the spare rooms. Now she could settle down to a quiet, restful afternoon.

And up at Rowett's Reserve a patch of glistening coals flushed red and pale alternately as the windy gusts swept over them in fierce ripples. For the log from Aunt Hester's campfire had burst into flame at daybreak, and now it was a long bed of incandescent ash and coal, hidden and almost smokeless in the midday haze of heat and dust. Miraculously it hadn't set fire to anything. The Reserve was swept clear of leaves and undergrowth by trampling feet and the wind, especially near the permanent fireplaces. Even at the edge where Aunt Hester had lit her forbidden campfire there was nothing but bare ground and dust for twenty or thirty yards. And so whenever a strong gust swirled bits of live ash and burning cinders downwind, they lay harmlessly in the dust, sending up

134

smoky little wisps now and then until they went out altogether or broke up and disappeared.

The Dragon was loose, but he couldn't find anything to devour.

Forty or fifty yards away beyond the boundary fence of The Big Scrub, where the trees grew tall and thick and the ground was littered with dry leaves and fallen branches, there was food, food, food, as far as the eye could see. But try as he might, straining his red tongue and stretching out the hot needles of his claws, the Dragon couldn't reach it . . . yet.

And nobody was aware of it. Nobody knew and nobody saw. Cars raced past on the highway nearby; trucks and buses ferried up and down. The danger could have been destroyed by a blow by one man, by a child. A bucket of water, a shovel of sand. But nobody knew, and so nothing was done.

Out on the plains on Ochre Flat, Mrs. Pine was hurrying to the C.W.A. meeting. She was late, but she guessed that many of the other women would be late too. The midday news bulletin was coming through on the car radio as she drove along; the temperature was a hundred and three—and still rising. There was a cool change on the way, the Weather Bureau announced hopefully, but it would probably take twenty-four hours to move in from the west. In the meantime the car bounced over ruts and the heat seemed to flow out from the shimmering stubble paddocks all around and sear the skin off her arm through the open window.

Suddenly she clicked her tongue impatiently; she had forgotten to let down the sliprails of Ginger's stall. Not that it was her fault. She'd have to speak to Crystal very sternly about this sort of thing; it was happening too often. Still, as the day had turned out, perhaps it was just as well. The water trough was full, there was plenty of food in the manger, and the straw thatch would keep the stable cooler than most places.

Then she remembered the cat. Old Puss'll-do was still curled up in the passage. She sighed. "Pets! The place is overrun with them," she said softly to herself. "Let's hope that old Puss'll-do has enough sense not to make a mess." She was frowning as she drove down the wide hot street of Ochre Flat and pulled up in front of the C.W.A. Hall.

At the Upper Gumbowie School the principal ordered the lunch bell to be rung early so that the children could escape from the boiling classrooms and try to find something cool to drink. He had already had three cases of heat prostration on his hands, and during the lunch hour Lemon, who was out doing yard duty in the heat, nearly became a fourth.

"We'll dismiss at three o'clock this afternoon," the principal said to Strarvy, "especially for the children on the bus run. Try to get them home by four."

But Resin and Turps, Don and Debby Dobson, Burp Heaslip, and Bridget O'Brien didn't mind the heat at all. They ran across the baking yard to the canteen, raced each other to the line, threw spinning bottle tops upwind, and chased one another until their faces looked like mottled blood plums and their hair stuck to the perspiration on their foreheads in little wet spikes.

"Whew!" Burp said, "it's hot."

"The hottest day this year, I reckon," Don agreed. "Easy."

And then the bell rang and they tried to flush their plum-purple cheeks under the taps before flopping to their desks again with their pants sticking to the seats

136

and the wet trickle of perspiration tickling the backs of their legs.

While the women at Ochre Flat were starting their meeting, and the children at Upper Gumbowie School were having their lunch break, and Aunt Hester in Summertown was preparing a cold salad for herself, the men of the Emergency Fire Service in all these places fidgeted at their work. If they were outside they kept glancing up at the horizon every few minutes, half expecting to see the smudge of smoke they dreaded. And if they were inside they found themselves listening tensely, half expecting to hear the wailing of sirens they feared. For this was a red-alert day, a peak emergency; fire-danger rating—serious; more than serious, explosive.

There was a total fire ban throughout the state, of course, but this was no guarantee of safety. On days like this it only needed one person to be careless, somewhere —a dropped cigarette butt, a cinder, a spark. And there were always careless people.

Just after midday the weather worsened. The temperature rose to a hundred and seven. The wind, laden with dust and grit, was sandpaper-harsh and needle-hot. And it came in fierce gusts and surges that swirled and eddied like willy-willies. Now, suddenly, one of these swept through Rowett's Reserve. In an instant the ash and cinders from Aunt Hester's campfire spiraled up, spun southward, and rained down into The Big Scrub like hot shrapnel. Soon little feathers of smoke streamed and wavered from the spots where they fell, like fumes escaping from silent valves in the earth. And a moment later sudden plumes of flame shot up in three different places—red and terrible blooms on the dried twigs and grassy tussocks. They spread with incredible speed. Within ten seconds the flames were as high as the treetops; within a minute the three fires had joined together in a common front; within five minutes a full-scale bushfire was roaring through The Big Scrub.

The Dragon was free!

The Dragon's rampage

It was hard to say who saw the smoke first. Some said it was Old Barnacle Bill, others said it was Strarvy. But it didn't matter because within a minute or two the telephone switchboards at Gumbowie and Summertown were jammed with calls. The sirens wailed urgently and the men of the Emergency Fire Service dropped whatever they were doing and ran to their fire trucks. As they did so they automatically turned their eyes to the north as if they knew already what message the wind had on its breath. Everybody else did the same; shopkeepers and bartenders in the town, farmers, carriers, and contractors in the country—all turned their heads to the north and stopped still for a moment. They were reading the story of the smoke.

A smudge as big as a mountain was spreading across the sky. It was the color of dirty sulfur and growing with terrible speed. They knew what that meant. The fire was already in The Big Scrub, with a wind like a blast furnace behind it. For fifty miles it had endless food to feed on. The country was rough, with no firebreaks and few good roads. The men knew what was happening. From miles around they came streaming in to give help, long before the special calls went out over the radios and telephones asking for volunteers. It was going to be the bitterest fight in years.

By two o'clock the first news started to come back to Gumbowie, but it was confused. The fire was traveling so fast that even the fire-control officers with their walkie-talkies couldn't get a very clear picture. But everyone knew that things were bad. The whole sky was dark now, and the sun was hidden by huge loops and swirls of copper-colored clouds. The air reeked of smoke. The fire was five miles wide, people said, and spreading quickly.

By half past two the reports were worse still. The wall of fire was ten miles wide and was roaring through The Big Scrub like an express train. Although ten E.F.S. Units and five hundred volunteers were now battling their hardest, they could barely make a mark. There was talk of abandoning The Scrub and trying to burn breaks out in the open stubble. But that meant giving up twenty or thirty miles of country without a fight.

At the Upper Gumbowie School the principal came in to Strarvy. "I think we'd better send the children home," he said. "Their parents will be getting anxious. Bus people first. As soon as you can."

"Yes, sir," Strarvy said.

When the teachers dismissed their classes soon after half past two, Resin, Turps, and Columbine came tumbling out and ran for the bus at the gate.

"Gosh! Look at the smoke!"

They all stopped short. "Jeepers!"

"I've never seen it like that before."

"Ugh! It hurts your nose."

"Your eyes and throat, too."

"What about the men trying to fight it? I'll bet some of them are nearly blind."

They were right. A few of the firefighters were straggling back into Gumbowie. Their eyes were red and sore. Some had damp handkerchiefs tied over their mouths and noses, but they coughed and rasped just the same. Two had been overcome by the heat and suffocating smoke and had to be helped into the Community Hall where the women of the town had set up an emergency bushfire center.

Some of the men were shouting to one another, "It's past Marble Gap! Nothing'll hold it now."

"We were in Conroy's Gully when it came thundering down the slope. Never seen anything like it. Lucky to get out alive."

"Makes a flamethrower look like a candle."

The children were agog and a little afraid. More and more truckloads of men streamed through the town. Now and then a car or a fire-control officer in a jeep tore past urgently.

Strarvy came running from the school, shepherding Lemon and calling the bus children to get on board.

"Hurry," he shouted.

He counted their heads quickly as they scrambled up the steps and flopped into their seats.

"Twenty-two, twenty-three, twenty-four . . ." He looked around in exasperation. "There's always someone missing. Who is it?"

141

"Burp, sir."

"I might have known. Where is he *this* time?"

"Over at the hall, sir."

"Whatever for?"

"Finding out about the fire I think, sir."

Strarvy climbed into the driver's seat, blew a loud blast on the horn, and started the engine. He was just starting to move off when Burp came catapulting out of the Community Hall, shot across the street, and swung himself on board.

"Sorry, sir," he panted, forestalling Strarvy's reprimand. "I was just checking on the fire."

"And what is the verdict, Captain?" Strarvy asked sarcastically.

Burp's forehead was wet with perspiration, and his freckles stood out pink and thick.

"Bad, sir. The men are retreating everywhere." He wiped his forehead with his shirt sleeve. "Gosh, the bus is hot, sir."

Strarvy revved up the engine and the bus lumbered off down the street. "It won't be so bad once we get moving."

"Even the wind's pretty hot, sir. And so full of smoke you can't breathe."

He was right. Even after they had gone a mile or two the inside of the bus was stifling. But if they opened the windows it was worse.

When they came to the first stop, Brenda Wilson's mother was waiting for her in the car. "I'll take Paula too," she said. "Mrs. Fritsche called me. We thought it best, with the fire the way it is. It's no day for them to be walking home from the bus."

So Brenda and Paula went off with Mrs. Wilson, and the bus ground on up the road. Visibility was getting worse and worse. The smoke, which until now had been streaming mainly above them, seemed to drop and blanket the land. Strarvy sat forward, peering anxiously through the windshield, driving as fast as he dared. Bridget O'Brien's stop loomed up around the next bend, but Strarvy wouldn't open the door to let her out. He turned anxiously to Lemon.

"We can't put her down in this," he said in a low voice. "Before long she won't be able to see her fingers in front of her face. Her parents'll be worried stiff."

Lemon agreed. "I don't think we should let anyone off the bus. Not until things get better."

"They won't get better, that's for certain. Not for a long time, anyway."

"What shall we do, then? There's no point in taking them back to school. It's probably locked up anyway."

Lemon looked back at the rows of hot, flushed faces behind her. "Bring them home," she said.

"Home?"

"To our place, Humpty Doo. We'll give them all a drink and settle them down comfortably until the danger is over. Then we can run them home afterward."

Strarvy looked approvingly at his new wife. "Good idea," he said, and drove off quickly down the Summertown road that led up past Humpty Doo, Bottlebrush Barn, Old Barnacle's store, and the wide straggling farms of the Pines, Heaslips, and Dobsons. It was only another nine or ten miles to Humpty Doo, but Strarvy soon saw how difficult the trip was going to be. The smoke grew thicker, the heat grew worse. Twice he nearly collided with trucks racing back the way they had come.

"It's sweeping down on Gumbowie," one of the drivers yelled. "We'll have the fight of our lives to save the town."

Strarvy accelerated and sent the old bus lurching forward.

"At that rate it won't be long before it cuts the road behind us," he said to Lemon, "but what about the track ahead?" Five miles further on he suddenly had his answer. The air was now thick with ash and drifting cinders, bits of blackened leaves and burnt grass, that were swept along and shredded by the wind. The stench of smoke swirled into the bus, filling the air with murk, and smarting in their eyes and throats.

Strarvy set his lips and drove on desperately. In his heart he was starting to be afraid; in his mind he was searching for advice, trying to remember a place where he and the children would be safe. All along the road on his right ran parts of The Big Scrub, sweeping up the slopes to the hilly land beyond; on the left there were trees too, but cleared paddocks every so often with fences and stubble and farmhouses as well.

They had just climbed out of the dry creek bed of the Bongabilly Soak and were straightening up on the level stretch of road a mile from Humpty Doo, when some of the children yelled.

"Look! Look!"

There was a babble of shrieks and cries, out of which Strarvy and Lemon heard only Burp's bellowing.

"Go for your life, sir! It's the fire!"

But Strarvy had already seen it. The whole crest of the slope above them suddenly boiled over with flame, as if a crimson sea had swept the top of the ridge and was tossing and leaping down the other side in wild waves of fire. Strarvy pressed the accelerator down hard and the bus roared down the road through the dust and stinking smoke. Forty, fifty, sixty miles an hour, with Strarvy crouching at the wheel and every bolt in the bus jarring and rattling. It was as fast as the bus would go.

On the right the fire poured down the hillside like burning gas from a tank. None of them—not even Strarvy or Lemon—had ever seen a big bushfire close at hand, and its horror stunned them. The noise was sickening, the sight unbelievable. Huge masses of flame like outbursts from the sun's rim broke away from the fire and shot high into the air, flapping and folding in fierce incandescent sheets. Whole trees exploded into torches. There was fire on the ground, and fire like hellish harpies in the air. The whole world was writhing and flinging, convulsing, twisting . . . and dying.

Up the road the bus flew, with the fire not a quarter of a mile away. Past the gates of Humpty Doo they shot, with Lemon pressing her hands to her head and crying out, "The house. Oh, my God, what about my things!" Between the two rows of big gum trees on either side of the road they rocketed, with the leaves twisting in the heat and the oil in them vaporizing like benzene.

"The fallow paddock, sir!" It was Burp's voice in Strarvy's ear again. "Turn into our gate, and head for the fallow paddock past the dam."

Strarvy had thought of it too. The only spot in the district, an oasis of earth in a world of fire, the Heaslips' ploughed paddock beckoned him on through the smoke and heat. The bus seemed as if it was about to burst into flame. Columbine and Debby had slumped in their seats; the big trees were blowing up like gunpowder behind them. But like an escaping colt with whips of fire cracking at its heels, the bus swung through the Heaslips' gate and tore down the track. Behind them the whole world had disappeared in smoke and flame—The Big Scrub and Humpty Doo, Barnacle's store and Bottlebrush Barn—all swallowed alike in the fiery holocaust. Almost beside them now, the fire was racing in the long stubble and grass of the Heaslips' paddock. Ahead lay the chocolate handkerchief of the fallow land they were straining to reach. But they didn't quite make their goal. A quarter of a mile inside the Heaslips' farm, where the track turned to skirt around the dam, Strarvy did what Mrs. Heaslip had always been saying someone would do. A tire, tormented by heat and angular gravel, suddenly burst with a bang. Strarvy instinctively swung the wheel, and the next moment the bus lurched off the track and headed straight for the dam. There was a flurry of wheels in mud, a squelching slide, and a final tremendous splash. Luckily the bus remained upright. There was a moment of stunned silence, then a babble of shouts and cries. Strarvy jumped quickly from the driver's seat and strode up the sloping center aisle.

"Everyone all right?"

"Ye-e-es."

There were a few jarred wrists and bruises, but no one was badly hurt.

"All out!" Strarvy ordered, trying to make a joke of it. "This is the special stop for today." The water was lapping the entrance steps, but it was only two feet deep, and one by one Strarvy and Lemon helped to shuffle the children to the shore.

"Wow!" Resin said, wading ahead and trying to cheer up Columbine, who was pale and exhausted. "What if the big blue crayfish gets Burp by the toe again?"

But there wasn't much laughter about anymore. The fire had swept past them and was now far ahead, break-

146

ing across the distant stubble in a low red wave. Behind them, and all around, was a world of smoke and blackness—black for cinders, black for ashes, and black for mourning. The smoke and stench still covered everything; and dotted all over the landscape like bitter red roses on the black earth were burning things—logs and fallen trees, stumps and limbs, fence posts and farm buildings.

Some were small and idly glowing, others were fountains of fire streaming with flame in the wind. Every now and then a tree crashed down on the slope of The Big Scrub with a wild shower of sparks like a gigantic Roman candle. The air was dirty with smoke and ash, the sky hidden. And now that the monster had rushed past and devoured everything, there was a strange silence, the ominous silence of desolation, like a landscape on the moon.

How long they lay sprawled on the bank of the dam no one knew. Perhaps they were a little lightheaded from the heat, the mad race with the fire, and the crash into the dam. They were a forlorn lot on their little unscarred island in the middle of the great ring of devastation; the bus with its rump stuck up in the air and its nose under the water like a fat old pig in a bath; all the barefooted dirty-faced children lolling about listlessly like shell-shocked refugees. And Lemon, her muddy shoes and stockings in a pitiful little heap beside her, and her eyes weeping from grief and smoke, burying her head in her hands and repeating over and over, "Our new home and all our lovely things! Our new home and all our lovely things!"

It may have been no more than an hour but it seemed a day before any other living creatures moved in that deserted land.

But at last they came—first a truck careering up the

147

burned-out road; then a car; and shortly afterward three cars and a jeep. Some of them stopped at the remains of Barnacle's store, some turned up the track to Bottlebrush Barn, and some raced straight past. Strarvy ran up the track toward the road, and the children stood up on the bank of the dam waving and yelling. One or two drivers saw them and swung down the track. Mr. Pine was among them driving a truck, with his wife following close behind in the car. He had been fighting the fire further up the Summertown road when the wind had suddenly swept it through his own farm; his wife had come hurrying back from the C.W.A. meeting at Ochre Flat but had not been able to get through the line of fire till now. They both jumped from their vehicles and ran toward the children. And Resin and Turps, dragging Columbine between them, hurried forward too.

"They're safe, Harry!" they heard their mother cry. "They're safe! They're safe!" Then she rushed up to them and grasped them, all three together, and held them so tightly that Columbine squeaked a protest: "Ow, Mum, you're hurting me! You're squeezing my arm!"

"Thank God," their mother was saying fervently, not as an answer to Columbine's squeak, but as a prayer of gratitude.

Other parents were rushing up too—Mr. and Mrs. Dobson, Mrs. O'Brien and Mr. Hammond, and even old Emil Eckert. Emil's face was black, his hair was half-singed from his head, and his eyes were the color of carrots. But nobody laughed at the way he looked. For Emil had fought with a heart like a lion. He had rescued two men from almost certain death when they had collapsed, by carrying them, one under each arm, back to the fire truck and driving them to safety. He was a hero, a Victoria Cross winner in his way, but he had lost everything he owned.

"At least d' childrens is safe," he said, sagging from exhaustion. "T'ank God for dat! One time we t'ink maybe d' fire has got dem too."

One by one the children were picked up and driven back to Gumbowie. By a desperate effort the town had been saved, all but two or three houses on the outskirts, and now a big relief plan was being organized to give food and shelter to the refugees from the fire.

"That accounts for them all," Strarvy said when the last carload had been driven off. "Now, there's only the bus."

"That'll have to wait," Mr. Pine said. "Till someone can pull it out tomorrow."

Mrs. Pine turned to Strarvy and Lemon. "You'd better come with us. We'll have to go to the Community Hall in Gumbowie."

Columbine was hanging on to his mother's hand. "Come on, Mum," he said. "I'm tired. Let's go home."

Mrs. Pine's eyes still seemed to be smarting from the fire. "Columbine," she said softly, "don't you understand? There is no home."

The aftermath

It was late in the afternoon. Fire trucks and police cars were still moving up and down the road, although the fire had been brought under control at last, far out on the cleared plains. But a hundred square miles of bush and farmland had been laid waste.

At Humpty Doo, Lemon stared unbelievingly at the ruin before her. Nothing remained, nothing but a few heaps of blackened stone and rubble. A fire truck had sprayed the smoldering ashes, but it was pointless because there was nothing left to be saved. Resin, Turps, and Columbine stood miserably at Mrs. Pine's side watching Lemon and Strarvy. They had stopped at Humpty Doo because Lemon had begged them to, but now everyone was sorry they had.

"All my wedding presents," Lemon was saying in a flat, grief-stricken voice. "My wedding dress and trousseau, my photos and clothing, and all our new furniture; even the crockery and saucepans. All gone! All gone!"

Strarvy, who was scuffing the ground with his shoe, picked up a bit of metal from the ashes. He turned it over in his palm.

"From the pupils of Upper Gumbowie School," he read. *"With best wishes."*

Strarvy stared at it for a minute, then threw it back into the ashes. "Our fireside chairs," he said bitterly. "Fireside is right."

Just then Lemon gave a cry of dismay. In the ruins of what had once been the veranda, she found a crushed and distorted bit of wire frame. It was the canary's cage. "Poor little fellow!" she cried. "What a horrible thing to do—to keep him in a cage so he couldn't escape. Locked up till he was burned alive."

Suddenly Turps turned to her mother, wide-eyed with horror. "Mum!" she said, trembling. "Did you let Ginger out of her stall this morning?"

It was the moment Mrs. Pine had been dreading. It was the reason she hadn't taken the children back to the ruins of Bottlebrush Barn, but had brought them straight from the dam with Strarvy and Lemon, leaving Mr. Pine to mourn their lost home alone. But Turps was gazing at her mother's face and reading it well enough.

"No!" she screamed. "No! No!" She broke away and started running back up the road.

"Crystal!" Mrs. Pine called severely. "Crystal, come back!"

But Turps didn't even hear her. Her mind was too full of the picture of a horse. A fear-crazed horse, locked in its stall and unable to escape, hurling itself against the rails in a mad frenzy as the flames roared down on it.

"Ginger!" she sobbed. "Ginger! Ginger!"

Her mother turned quickly to Resin. "Melton, run and stop her! You *must* stop her!"

"He won't be able to, Mrs. Pine," Strarvy said. "Not now that she realizes what has happened. Better follow her in the car."

They caught up with Turps halfway back to Bottle-brush Barn. Mrs. Pine slowed down and called to her. "Come on, dear; get into the car."

"Not . . . not unless you promise to take me back," Turps sobbed. "Not unless you promise."

"Don't be so silly, dear. Come on, you'll wear yourself out this way."

"Promise."

"Very well then. But . . . but you must . . . "

Mrs. Pine didn't seem able to say what Turps must, because she left the sentence unfinished as she drove in between the charred stumps of the gateposts and pulled up near the ruined house.

It was a pitiful sight. A few columns of smoke still rose around the burned-out yard, and the stench of destruction was acrid in their nostrils. Resin and Columbine couldn't believe what they saw. Their lovely house, with the wide verandas and morning-glory creeper, just didn't exist anymore. Only a few blackened walls and the remnants of a brick chimney stood up in the gathering evening shadow. Everything else was gone—the kitchen and the bedrooms, the cupboards and shelves, beds, blankets, and toys—all the things that had been so friendly and permanent that very morning when they had run out to catch the bus were now suddenly gone, changed in a flash into ashes and bits of soot. But Turps didn't even seem to have noticed these things. She sprang from the car and raced across the fire-swept ground toward the spot where the stable had been. Halfway across she stopped and cried out in horror. Her father, who had been doing something nearby with the rifle and shovel he always kept in the truck, heard the cry and ran to intercept her.

"You shouldn't have come, Crystal!" he said. "You shouldn't have come!"

A shape was lying in the ruined stable—a shape like a mound, charred and horrible, among the fire-blackened stone and twisted sheets of iron.

"Is she . . . did she . . . did she . . . ?" She couldn't bring herself to say it. Her father didn't speak for a minute, but she could see the despair in his eyes. Then he shook his head faintly.

"No," he said. "She . . . she didn't get away."

"Oh, Daddy! Daddy!" She clung to him with her face pressed against his torn and sooty shirt, sobbing hysterically. "It . . . it was all my fault! If . . . if I'd let her out this morning, like Mummy said, she'd still be . . . be alive." And she went on with her wild fit of sobbing. Her father put his grimy arm around her shoulders, but he knew there was no comforting her, so he turned slowly and led her back to the car. His own heart was too full of loss and hopelessness for him to help anyone—not even Turps.

Meanwhile, the others had made their own tragic discoveries. In a corner of the house paddock there was a great pile of smoking carcasses, more than a hundred of them. They were the dead bodies of sheep. Panic-stricken, crazy with pain and fear, the flock had stampeded into the fences and died there slowly and horribly with their wool on fire. Now they were nothing but bloated and blackened lumps, noisome and horrible, lying heaped together, the stumps of their legs sticking up grotesquely. And the stinking smoke, the stench of death and burnt flesh, rose over everything.

Under the blackened wire netting of the rabbit hutch, Resin found the charred bodies of Fluff and Tuft. He ran over to the remains of Pinch's cage, but couldn't see anything. The whole framework had collapsed and he was afraid to probe too closely because he knew well enough what he would find. Turkeys, fowls, pet lambs, and calves had perished.

Columbine looked about, awestruck. "Where . . . where's Puss'll-do?" he asked.

Resin saw a chance of offering some comfort among the ashes. "Oh, he'll be all right; probably shot off down to the creek or the banks of the dam."

"D'you reckon?"

"Sure to have! No need to worry about him."

Though numbed by her sense of loss and despair, Mrs. Pine felt a catch in her throat. She glanced quickly at the ruins of the house, but then looked away again, afraid that Columbine might have noticed her. Poor Puss'll-do. She had left him locked in the house.

Though she had tried to keep the news from the children, the thought of big, friendly old Puss'll-do trapped in the burning house was the final agony. Her breath caught in a sob, and she turned away so that they couldn't see her face.

Mr. Pine joined them, and they all stood silently together in the gathering shadow. A black world ringed them around: Black, black, black! Black for mourning, black for death.

Their mother was the first to rouse herself. She drew the back of her hand across her eyes and looked at the children.

"Well," she said, trying to sound lighthearted, but only succeeding in embarrassing them instead. "We'd better go. No use staying here."

For the first time it seemed to dawn on Columbine that there was no such thing as "home" anymore. He opened his eyes like marbles. "Where are we going to sleep?"

His father left Turps, who was still sobbing silently, and walked over to the car. "In Gumbowie," he said. "They've set up a relief depot there."

"Will there be lots of people?"

"Yes, lots."

"Who?"

"The Dobsons."

"Don and Debby? Was their house burned too?"

"Yes, and so was the Fritsches' and the O'Reillys' and the Eckerts'."

"Will they all be in Gumbowie?"

"I guess. Unless they've gone somewhere else to stay."

"And Strarvy and Lemon too?"

"Yes."

"And Old Barnacle Bill?"

Mr. Pine's face was sad. "No, not Old Barnacle."

They could sense something bad, something terrible. Even Turps lifted her head and waited, hushed.

"Why not?" Columbine asked at last.

"He . . . he was burned to death today—in his shop."

There was another silence, a shock of unbelief. Resin seemed to be working the muscles of his throat to get the words out. In the end not much more than a whisper came. *"Burned to death?"*

"Yes, the police found him while you were at Humpty Doo."

"Bushfires! It's always bushfires! Every summer it's

155

bushfires! I *hate* them! I *hate* them! I *hate* them!" It was
Turps. She was holding on to the side of the car and
pummeling the hood with her fist. "Every year it's the
same. Now they've killed Ginger! They've killed Ginger,
and all the pets, and the sheep! And even poor old Barnacle. And burned everything in his shop. It makes me
sick! Why don't we go and live in the town . . . ?" And
she burst into sobs.

Everybody was miserable and uncomfortable. But Mr.
Pine led Turps firmly to the car door, opened it, and sat
her inside. The others were about to follow when suddenly there was the sound of clawing and scrabbling from
the roof of the old underground tank, a scuttling blur
across the intervening ground, and the next moment something landed *plop* on Resin's hip and skittered up onto
his shoulder.

"Pinch!" The cry went up all around. "Pinch! Where
in the world have you come from?"

"From the tank," Mr. Pine said. "He must have
climbed in under the roof and hung from the rafters by
his claws or his tail."

"But how did he get out of his cage?"

"Providence, I guess. Perhaps the cage was smashed
by a falling branch or beam."

"Pinch! Oh, you poor old boy." Resin was stroking his
fur and rubbing his stomach at the same time. "Oh, he's
frightened! He's trembling! Look! And his fur is all
singed! Just smell it."

"Poor fellow! But at least he's alive." Mr. Pine looked
across the blackened slope. "I wonder how many of his
mates in The Big Scrub even managed that!"

"What are we going to do with him, Dad? We can't
leave him here. He'll starve."

156

"We'll just have to take him with us."

"Can we? Gosh, thanks, Dad."

"Come on, then. It'll be dark soon."

Strarvy and Lemon had already gone into Gumbowie with the Dobsons. For some time cars and trucks had been moving up and down the Summertown road through the bushfire-blackened country, but now one of them suddenly turned off and came racing up the track toward them. Before it had stopped they knew who it was.

Aunt Hester came tumbling out, gabbling and clacking, while Uncle Stan was still turning off the ignition switch.

"Oh, you poor dear," she cried, rushing over to Mrs. Pine and throwing her sticklike arms around her. "Oh, what you must have been through!" She called to Uncle Stan in a gush of commiseration.

"Oh, just look at their house, Stanley! Just look at their house!"

Resin felt certain that later on she would be using the same exclamations when giving her exciting eyewitness account during afternoon tea at the Summertown Ladies' Tennis Club.

"Everything?" she was saying in her high-pitched gush. "You lost everything?"

"Everything," Mr. Pine said bitterly. "Everything down to the last fence post and knothole."

"But, Harry, what are you going to do? What *are* you going to do?"

"Work! Find a job in Adelaide or Melbourne even, until I can scrape up a bit of money again. But it'll be a long haul."

Even Uncle Stan was appalled. "But that'll take years."

"Twenty years—to get the farm back the way it was."

"Twenty years!" Uncle Stan scratched his nose unnecessarily. "Gosh! Resin and Turps will be thirty years old by then."

"It'll be their job in the end, I guess. I'll be too old to finish it."

Aunt Hester was afraid the men were stealing her thunder, so she piped up on a new subject. "Where are you going to sleep tonight?"

"We thought in Gumbowie. They're setting up a relief depot in the hall."

But Aunt Hester wouldn't hear of it.

"What nonsense, Muriel! Sleeping in a hall with all sorts of other people! You're coming home with us and that's that!"

Mrs. Pine was very grateful. In spite of her crust and fuss, Aunt Hester was generous at heart.

"Thank you, Hester. That would be lovely. But there are five of us."

"No bother, Muriel. We had five staying over the weekend. My cousin Harold and his family just left this morning. It won't take a minute to put up the beds again."

Under Aunt Hester's overpowering organization they were about to get into the cars to drive to Summertown when Resin happened to move in front of the others.

"Melton?" Aunt Hester said, suddenly suspicious. "What's *that*?"

Resin knew he was trapped. "It's . . . it's . . . Pinch."

"The *possum*!" Aunt Hester's question was really a screech.

"It's all right, Aunty. He's very frightened and burned. He won't hurt anyone."

But Aunt Hester was adamant. "Melton," she said severely, "you are not bringing that creature. I just will not have it in the house."

Turps tried to interpose, then, and even Mrs. Pine got as far as "But, Hester . . . "

"It'll die, otherwise," Turps said bitterly, "like everything else."

"*No!*" Aunt Hester insisted. "I'm sorry! No possum!"

Resin suddenly felt a hot wave of resentment and defiance sweeping up his face. "Then I'm not coming either."

"Melton!" His mother was scandalized.

"Well, gosh, you can't leave him here to die! I'll sleep in the hall in Gumbowie, then!"

Mr. Pine could see that a crisis was threatening. Everyone was exhausted and numb from the day's disaster. It was plain that Resin would not give in. "You couldn't keep him in a hall full of people, Resin," he said quietly. "It just wouldn't work."

"Well, what'll I do?" Resin said doggedly. "I'm *not* going to leave him here."

"Give him to me. I'll lock him in the cabin of the truck. Tomorrow we'll see what we can do for him."

"But are you going to leave the truck here?"

"No. I'll follow you up to Summertown. Mum can drive the car."

Uncle Stan prepared to lead the way. "You saved the two vehicles, Harry—the car and the truck?"

"Yes. I was using one and Mum had the other. So we saved those two—those, and the clothes we've got on our backs."

For ten miles they drove through a madman's landscape. It was dark now, but the whole world, from horizon to horizon, glowed and smoked like an endless,

159

gloomy inferno. Along the ridges the skyline was etched out in trees of fire. All over the ranges of The Big Scrub the burning stumps stood in columns and pillars of gleaming coals. Far, far across the land red spear points of light glared like evil eyes, winking and flaring. High branches fell in rivers of fire, tossing up a wild surf of flame and sparks in the face of the night. Fence posts for miles along the sides of the road burned and smoldered, and sometimes whole columns of them marched up the sides of the hills in long files. And over everything lay the acrid stench of smoke, a stinking smell of black and charred and wasted earth. It was a drive that no one would ever forget.

But at last they broke clear of the fire-devastated waste, and drove on to Summertown. Aunt Hester bustled to get everyone settled.

"You poor dears! You poor dears!" she kept repeating. "Whatever are you going to do now?"

But Resin, Turps, and Columbine were too tired to take much notice of her, and their parents were more interested in the news coming over the radio. Thirty-three houses were in ruins, and five people were known to have died in the fire—Old Barnacle, and a family of four from Echo Gully, up in The Big Scrub. The town of Upper Gumbowie had barely been saved; ten thousand sheep were dead, and so were hundreds of cattle, horses, pigs, poultry, and other livestock. Wildlife had perished too. And every farm from Gumbowie to Ochre Flat was a black waste, a bitter desert.

Aunt Hester came fussing in with cool drinks.

"What beats me," she said loudly, "is how these fires start. They never seem to be able to find out."

"There's a person behind it, you can be sure of that,"

Uncle Stan said. "Some silly numskull with no more brains than a radish."

"Well, I hope they find out who started this one," Aunt Hester said. "And put him behind bars for a while."

Uncle Stan agreed. "Jail would be too good for him. An iron plowseat full of hot coals—that's what they ought to make him sit on."

Aunt Hester's jewelry bounced delightedly at that. "Yes, hot coals from his own bushfire. He wouldn't forget that in a hurry."

Uncle Stan looked at his angular wife thoughtfully. "I wonder if they'll ever find out who started it."

Outside a southerly gust plunged under the eaves, and a flurry of big flat raindrops came typing their message across the roof. Everyone ran to the windows. Resin and Turps yelled together.

"The change! The cool change! It's here!"

It was true. There was a second, stronger gust and the staccato rattle of heavy rain on iron roofs. Mr. Pine turned away slowly.

"Thank God for that," he said quietly. "But it's half a day too late."

The rain swept across the Gumbowie hills, and the landscape writhed and seethed. Pillars of white smoke stood up all over the slopes and valleys; twining scarves like white mist wreathed around the remnants of logs and trees. It rained on, drenching the land, choking the last lick of flame, dousing each secret, smoldering coal. It rained through the night, cool and soft, as if the weather was now trying to spread salve over the ruins of Bottlebrush Barn, the grotesque carcasses of the sheep, the dead

161

body of Ginger. But there was a scar across the land that would take years to heal.

Under the whiplash of the rain and the cool rush of the wind the February Dragon faltered, crouched low, and slunk away. Before long he was gone—hidden mysteriously, driven back to his cage. But he was not destroyed.

He was just waiting for another chance.

He is waiting now.

Format by Joyce Hopkins
Set in 11 pt. Times Roman.
Composed, printed and bound by Vail-Ballou Press, Inc.
HARPER & ROW, PUBLISHERS, INCORPORATED